Wild Horse, Wild Heart

A Bear Dance Ranch Novel: #2

Christina Rhoads

Wild Horse, Wild Heart
Copyright © 2019 Christina Rhoads
All rights reserved.

ISBN: (ebook): 978-1-949931-03-7
(print): 978-1-949931-04-4

Inkspell Publishing
5764 Woodbine Ave.
Pinckney, MI 48169

Edited By :Audrey Bobak
Cover Art By Najla Qamber

CHRISTINA RHOADS

DEDICATION

I have had the incredible pleasure of meeting some very fine horsewomen, and they have shaped the characters in this book, as well as my own relationships with horses and humans. I would especially like to thank Nancy Kleiner who taught me, from a very early age, what it meant to be fiercely independent and courageous when faced with challenges. Mary Miller Jordon for proving that our minds, hearts and horses can synchronize. Madison Shambaugh that dreams are meant to be big and scary (it's a good thing!!) and Stacy Westfall for her beautiful ride on her black mare. I have goosebumps just thinking about it!

I would also like to thank my mother, who encouraged my imagination to run free on the back of my pony, and drove me to all those riding lesson. I hope she doesn't mind that I'm writing about sexy cowboys?

Of course this book would not have happened without the AW girls. Thanks for being my rock(s)!!

And I must thank the man who each day makes me smile, laugh and hope for another magical year—all while offering hands-on inspiration for some of my favorite scenes ;)

CHRISTINA RHOADS

PROLOGUE

Corbin Darkhorse loosened the cinch and then pulled the saddle from Nighthawk's back. Using a thick towel, he rubbed dry the horse's dark coat. Sundays evenings, he thought, were always the hardest. He opened the bottle of liniment and poured a liberal amount into his palm, then cupped both hands around animal's leg and worked his fingers over the stretch of finely shaped tendons from shoulder to coronet band. As he straightened up, he could smell locust blooms. His heart began to beat too fast and he tried to remind himself he always felt this way around the anniversary of the accident—it would be ten years next week.

"Too close to forget and too long ago to fix." He spoke to Nighthawk. The gelding looked back at him and then flicked his long, dark tail. He knew he was being morose, but there was that scent again. Locust trees only lined the rivers further south, he reminded himself. It was, as usual, all in his head.

The horse snorted. It was time to get on the road. He opened the horse trailer door and loaded the animal, making sure the hay bag was filled with fresh alfalfa and deep pine shavings covered the floor. As he walked to his truck, the sun did a fast dip behind the mountains to the west and then disappeared completely. He had to smile at his own ridiculously large face plastered on the side of the horse trailer. Shaking his head, he remembered how proud he'd been picking it up from the dealership.

Inside the practically new truck, he keyed in an address on the GPS. Out of the corner of his eye, he saw the hostess from his Horsemanship clinic walking toward his vehicle. He kept his head down and he looked at his phone, hoping she would walk past. Of course, she tapped on his window. He rolled it down and put on his brightest horse-trainer-with-all-the-moves smile.

"Mr. Darkhorse," she said.

"Please, call me Corbin," he reminded her reflexively.

"*Corbin*, I really wish you would stay. It's late to be on the road and you worked so hard this weekend."

"Part of the job." He was trying to be professional.

"Well. Just so you know, all of us are so grateful that you come up to our little ranch to help us with our horses. And we, well, I, would like to repay you." The woman touched his arm and he knew what she meant.

Her fingers lingered, brushing over his bare skin where he had rolled his sleeves up. Maybe if he had not smelled the locust blossoms just minutes before, he would have relented and said yes. After all, he had many times before. But tonight was different; the restlessness of guilt and the anniversary of his cowardice were weighing upon him too heavily. He touched his hat. "I'm afraid I can't, ma'am. I have to pick up my mustang for the training competition in the morning."

She made a pouty face and touched his arm twice more before he was able to roll up his window and escape into the growing dusk.

Hours later, the sky fully dark and the road empty in front of him, he let his mind wander back to another all-night drive ten years prior. She had sat beside him that night, on the bench seat, singing along to the radio and talking in that quick way she did when she was excited. From the glow of the dash lights, he imagined her outline in the cab of his truck. They had pictured this life together; the one he was living: on the road teaching clinics, training horses, showing all over the country. They had dreamed the dust and sweat and adventure. He had been the coward who fled after nearly getting her killed.

The night opened before his truck and trailer, and as he drove into the darkness, he prayed for the first time in too long. A second chance was all he wanted. He knew he didn't deserve it, but yet he asked anyway.

CHRISTINA RHOADS

CHAPTER ONE

The wild horse reared and then lunged toward Elsie. She stepped back just as the mustang crashed into the steel stock panels. A cloud of dust enveloped her and the horse; for several long moments, they were alone in a world of golden haze.

The mustang stood perfectly still, breathing hard. She could see fear and anger in his eyes; she felt her own heart beating with similar anguish. Very slowly, she reached out her hand, hoping the horse would sniff her damp fingers.

"You always draw the crazy ones," she heard from behind her. The golden moment disappeared as the dust settled and the noise of the stockyard rushed to flood her ears. The mustang spun away from Elsie and she pulled her hand back.

She didn't want to turn and see the man standing behind her. At the sound of his voice, she was again seventeen, and falling in love for the first time.

A trickle of sweat made its way down her back and she forced her fisted hands to open at her sides.

Finally, she did turn, but only after straightening her shoulders and smoothing her face of any emotion. Corbin Darkhorse stood taller and broader than she remembered.

There was a smug smile on his expressive lips.

"You look good, Elsie," Corbin said. "You're training horses again?" He stared at her with his dark eyes and that slow, suggestive smile she remembered all too well. For a long moment, Elsie looked into his eyes, then her mind switched on and she jerked away, swallowing a mouthful of dirty words.

She turned back to the horse she had just signed up to train over the course of the next three months. What was wrong with her, she wondered, as she tried to not imagine how easily the terrified animal could stomp her to death with one of its four hooves. The last thing she wanted was *him* to see her nervous and second-guessing herself. What were the chances that she would run into her ex-sweetheart after almost ten years, and on the most stressful day of her career? She caught herself running her hand down her leg, feeling the long, puckered scar through the fabric of her jeans. She tried not to picture the rod of titanium holding her bones together, or the numerous pins and screws carefully placed so she could walk. She hoped when she turned back around he would be gone, and she would realize her imagination had conjured him out of the dust-filled air.

"Elsie, did you read my letters?" His voice was low and intimate despite the noisy stockyard.

The dust stung her eyes and made it hard to breathe. She didn't have to answer him. She owed him nothing.

"Okay, lady. Back your horse trailer up and let's get that mustang loaded," said a man wearing a tan cowboy hat. His belly appeared to be held up by his gold-rimmed belt buckle.

This was her moment to escape. She could jump into her '79 Chevy truck and tear out of the gravel parking lot, leave Corbin and the mustang behind her. She knew no one would fault her for changing her mind; this was a huge undertaking, to train a wild horse to be able to compete in just three short months. She peeked back into the pen; the horse stood with his head held high and black coat slick with sweat. His delicate ears swiveled, on the lookout for possible danger.

"So, are you taking the horse or not?" the man said. He looked down at his clipboard then up to meet Elsie's eyes. "Look, young woman. That's a heck of a mustang to draw. He's a wild one, for sure, and there's no shame in backing down and letting a more experienced man show him who's boss."

"Maybe I should take that horse for you," Corbin said. He moved to stand at the corral gate and stared at the black mustang. "I don't want to see you get hurt, Elsie. Again." He said the last part quieter, so just she could hear. He was too real.

Elsie felt her insides turn to fire; her lips came together in a straight, hard line. She knew all too well how the men around her thought they were better with horses than she—especially since her accident. In her experience, most of the so-called horse trainers would beat the animals into submission, then they would go around bragging about their abilities to anyone stupid enough to pay to go to one of their clinics. Womanizing blowhards, she thought, and there was no evidence to the contrary that Corbin Darkhorse was any different from all the rest.

"I'll back my rig in," Elsie said. "I do appreciate you helping a 'little woman' like me out with your advice and all, but I'm taking that horse home." She truly hoped her sarcasm was not lost on the dim man with the belt or arrogant Corbin Darkhorse.

Her eyes were bright with angry tears as she looked from the horse and back at the two men. All three males stared at her, the two humans with annoyed intrigue and the equine with worried anticipation. She gathered her courage and walked away from them. Her brown hair pulled free of her long braid and danced in the wind as she headed to her parked truck. She willed her hands to stay at her sides. Who cared if her hair was free and wild, she told herself, who cared if she looked younger and more feminine with it blowing in the wind, who cared if her limp was more pronounced when she hurried.

There was nothing she hated more than being told to move over and let a man do something she could do better. She wondered, for a brief moment, why she must always be at war with the world around her. Of all the places to run into Corbin Darkhorse, the stockyards—while she picked up a wild horse—was the last place she'd hoped to encounter him. Sometimes, at night after her accident, she had lain in bed and imagined beating Corbin at a horse show, on the rodeo circuit, or maybe at a colt-starting competition. In her mind, she had watched his face turn sad and sorry and she had heard him apologize for leaving her so abruptly. Of course, in her fantasy, she coolly thanked him, her eyes chill and smile barely touching the corners of her lips.

She reached her truck and pulled hard on the door. It grudgingly opened with a metal-on-metal screech. There was no time to recap her old love affair.

Her heart pounded as she threw the truck into gear and used her mirrors to back down the alley to the loading chute. She had to stop twice to wipe her sweating palms on her pant leg.

The gates opened and her new mustang came barreling down the chute. The big black horse pinned his ears flat back on his head and his coat caught the rays of morning sunshine. He was followed by a cloud of dust, kicked up by his hooves. Her breathing quickened because he was a beautiful and wild sight. The horse stopped just at the threshold of her trailer and snorted, lowering his head. The wild horse gathered his haunches and leaped into the trailer. Her new adventure had just begun.

She slammed shut the heavy stock gate and tried to ignore Corbin. She could feel his eyes on her back and wished she had a sharp comment to yell before she climbed into her truck. Corbin said something to the older cowboy and Elsie turned around and stared at the two men, one old and heavy and the other young and lean.

"What did you say?" she demanded.

"Oh, nothing," the older cowboy said.

"I don't want to see you get hurt," Corbin replied. "I'd like to have at least a little bit of competition at the Mustang Championship."

"Oh, really?" Elsie replied. "You're so confident that you have it in the bag, even though you haven't even touched your mustang?"

"Well," he said. "I just know my way around a horse. I know how they think, they act, what they like, they fear. I just have a way with horses is all." He shrugged his shoulders as if he were modest.

"You arrogant man!" Her whole face felt hot and tight with anger. How dare he assume that he could gentle a wild horse better than she?

He threw his head back and laughed and then stared right at Elsie. She saw that his eyes were still the most beautiful deep brown, shot through with flecks of green.

"Elsie, you haven't changed at all. You're still all fire." He looked down and then back up and his face was soft and eyes very clear as he spoke in barely more than a whisper. "Let me take you to dinner and explain."

"Like hell, Corbin. See you in the winner's circle, and you can tell me what second place feels like!" She pulled on the door handle of her truck. Of course, it stuck a little but she managed to get it open and jumped inside before she said something truly unprofessional.

She turned the key and pumped the gas pedal, and the truck roared to life. In her rearview mirror, she could see Corbin. What a stupid man. What had she been thinking to fall for him all those years ago?

Corbin Darkhorse shoved his hands in his pockets. For the past ten years, he had imagined meeting Elsie

Rosewood, but never in his daydreams had the conversation gone so badly. He'd forgotten how easily she could get under his skin and make him say things he regretted.

"That's one hell of a girl," the stockyard man said. "Old girlfriend?"

"More than that," Corbin answered.

He followed the steel panels down to the pen holding a large gray gelding. The horse turned and gave him a hard stare and then moved to the opposite end of the corral. "You're not the only one less than pleased to see me today." Corbin spoke almost under his breath. The horse seemed unimpressed by his self-indulging pity. After being on the road, conducting so many clinics, Corbin had grown accustomed to people, especially women, meeting him with a mixture of awe and flirtation. Elsie had not exhibited either and seemed annoyed that he was even still alive. Of course, his guilt did not help.

"I know you didn't sign up for this," Corbin said to the horse. "But we better figure out how to get along."

The mustang flicked his ears back and Corbin smiled despite himself. He did love a good challenge and this horse looked like he would give him just that. A gust of wind brought the smell of manure, hay, and horse sweat to his nose. He rested his elbows on the rails and looked at the horses in other pens. His mind drifted back to Elsie as he mulled over their failed conversation. She had appeared like a blip on his radar and suddenly he could feel his pulse beating with new intensity. He'd known it was her as soon as he saw the long, brown braid and her slender form. Of course, he thought, she had drawn the black horse with wild, wild eyes and the flare of red in his nostrils. That girl had always attracted lightning, fire, and crazy horses. She was as wild as the mustangs just brought in from the range and Corbin couldn't believe that she was here, back on the circuit, and back in his life. He had wanted to follow her, jump in his truck, and chase her down. Make her listen to him, look at his face, and really listen to his words. He knew she was the type of woman who could only truly understand him if she listened with her heart. He had to make her understand why he had fled in sheer terror all those years ago, when she lay torn and broken in the hospital bed. If he didn't, if he couldn't get her to comprehend his reasons, then there would never be any hope of forgiveness from her. He knew he would have to open up his own sorry mess of a head to Elsie, somehow show that his heart was good and maybe even a little better than it had been ten years prior. At least he had convinced himself that it was better than before.

Of course, he had not known at first why he had run. It had taken nearly eight years after her accident. That was a long time to gallop, as if the hounds of hell were at his very heels. When he stopped, and found himself astride a horse in Australia, he had faced up and the dogs had backed down. Now those silly mutts slunk around draped in guilt. Seeing her standing on both her legs had helped ease some of it. Seeing her standing next to that crazy, black horse had made him all sorts of protective. He had wanted to hand her the reins of his most broke-saddle horse, keep her safe and tucked up on a gentle animal with no fire blowing out of its black nostrils.

The big gray lowered his head and stood watching Corbin. It was good, he reasoned, that he had not followed her. They would have fought. She would've yelled at him and kicked at his shins. He would've tried to grab her slender shoulders and hold her long enough to tell his limping story and who knew if it would have moved her? He'd built his living around words, teaching middle-aged women about horses with his little snippets of cowboy poetry. They loved him, all those women at his clinics, but Elsie was not one to buy into pretty words dancing around the truth.

The horse took two slow steps toward him, and Corbin let his wrists relax and his hands dangle free on the inside of the corral. He knew how to wait. Perhaps, he thought, that was what he would do, just wait. Let her come to him. Surely she knew who he was. His expensive truck and horse trailer, with his face plastered on the side, were sitting in the parking lot and it was hard to pick up a horse magazine and not see an article about his methods of gentling and training. Somehow, not completely through his own doing, he had become a sort of poster child for the natural horsemanship movement that was washing through the horse world. He suspected a lot his popularity had to do with his dark skin, black hair, and the legacy of his mother's people.

Who was he kidding? He smiled to himself. He knew Elsie would never come to him, especially since he had become so popular. He had to hope that fate would line them up again.

The gray horse lowered his head and sniffed the ground. His eyes were a bit softer than they had been ten minutes earlier. "Second Chance." His voice was low but the horse pricked his ears forward. "Can I call you that?" Corbin let the last bit of tension ease from his shoulders. "I'd like one of those myself."

With a big sigh, the mustang snorted, blowing a puff of dust across the dry pen.

Corbin looked up into the cloudless sky. A hawk wheeled high overhead. If fate didn't provide the time, he decided, he would have to go find her, but he would be ready this time. He would have his words lined up and his eyes clear so she could see all the way to his heart.

***

Elsie put the truck in gear and pulled away from the stockyards. Taking a deep lungful of clean air, she tried to calm her rapidly beating heart and concentrate on driving the horse trailer with her wild cargo in the back. Seeing Corbin had thrown her mind into a whirl of doubt and anger. Suddenly, she was terrified she'd made the wrong choice by pinning her future on the outcome of this wild horse training competition. Carefully, she loosened her grip on the steering wheel; breathe, she told herself. After her accident, during those first few months, one of the things that had given her courage was thinking about beating Corbin Darkhorse at a horse training competition. Forgiveness had never been one of her strengths.

***

Home was a rented patch of ground, more dust or mud—depending on the season—than anything else. She lived in her horse trailer, not in the horse part, but in the front where there were a cowboy shower and tiny bed. A propane stove and a sink with running water, so long as she remembered to fill the tank when she was in town.

She pulled off the dirt road and backed the trailer up to the round corral where she would leave her new mustang for the night. The corral walls were eight feet tall in case he got homesick and tried to jump out.

Nothing happened when Elsie opened the back door of the horse trailer. She had expected to see an explosion of wild horse. Holding the door wide with her boot, she peeked around to see the horse standing with his head down, sniffing the air. His matted mane and forelock fell forward, covering his left eye, and when he saw her watching, he raised his head and stared back. He had the wariness of a creature whose life had changed inexplicably over the past few months. She knew he had been rounded up from his family, castrated, and then assigned a human, all without any say on his part. The mustang looked as if he was trying to decide if she were friend or foe.

"C'mon, boy, I know it's a far cry from the mountains and meadows you used to roam with your family, but really, I'm all you have now. You and me, we have to bond and become best friends over the next few months—we don't have a choice." After years of training horses, she didn't think it even a little odd to be talking to the animal in such a frank fashion. Why not be honest with the horse?

Elsie's words to the mustang were true. Either she had to train this horse and win some money in order to make a name for herself, or she would have to go live with her mother and go to nursing school like her two older sisters. Being a nurse was a meaningful job; the problem was Elsie's heart ran free on the back of a horse. She had no idea how she could survive inside a building all day. She wished, not for the first time, that she was put together differently. Yet no matter how hard she tried, she couldn't leave behind her dream of working with horses. This was her last attempt to make a name for herself and hopefully put down a little bit of money on a small barn and arena all her own. If she was going to make it as a horse trainer, she needed clients who would send her their well-bred horses to train. Elsie knew very well that people only wanted to give horses to trainers with fancy titles and big winnings. Without the distinction of Mustang Champion, she was just another nobody-horse trainer, except, to make it worse, she had a gimpy leg.

The wild horse was in the same situation as Elsie, though he may not have realized it. More and more horses where being removed by the Bureau of Land Management to let cows graze the land and people build houses. This horse had two choices: one, he could fight Elsie all the way and she would have to send him back as an unbroken horse. There he would live in a pen for the rest of his life, or worse, he would be slated for euthanasia or sold by the pound for slaughter. Or, the option she was praying the horse chose: he could become a well-adjusted saddle horse and Elsie's companion, and the two of them could be ambassadors for the American Mustang. If he took the second choice, he wouldn't be free but he would be well loved and cared for and he would have her as his partner for life. Together, she hoped, the two of them could launch her career.

Elsie took a deep breath and exhaled. She wanted to convey all of this to the scared horse.

Just then, Sky, her retired reining horse, ambled over to see the newcomer in the trailer. The old horse leaned his pretty face with the full blaze over the corral gate and gave a welcoming whinny. The mustang snorted and launched himself in one quick leap out of the trailer and into his corral. He landed near the center of the pen and stood surveying the old horse, Elsie, and his new home. He didn't look impressed.

"I know, I know. It's not much. But this place isn't permanent. We are headed to bigger and better things, you and me." Elsie hoped she sounded confident.

Both horses lifted their heads as a black SUV pulled in next to Elsie's beat-up truck. Out stepped Earl, her landlord.

"Elsie," Earl said. He rested a hand on the hood of his very shiny vehicle and looked at the wild horse. "Is that a mustang?"

"Yes, he is," Elsie said. "I'm thinking of calling him Magic, what do you think?"

"Have you lost your ever-loving mind, girl?" Earl said. "You're going to get your fool-headed ass trampled to death by that horse. Look at those eyes. That horse is wild and he intends to stay that way."

Elsie did not completely disagree with Earl's statement. The horse did have wild eyes, but she took great pride in her horsemanship and so the rest of his pronouncement made her blood heat.

"Earl, you don't know a damn thing about horses. I'm training this mustang and that's the end of it." Elsie put both hands on her hips, threw her shoulders back, and glared at her landlord.

"Elsie," Earl said. His voice was gentler now, and he removed his sunglasses and looked away to the south. "I just sold this piece of land you've been renting. There's a natural gas reserve under here and so I sold the mineral rights. You know I need the money with my construction business not doing so well and the divorce and all."

Elsie was at a loss for words. She looked at the wild horse she had just brought home and at her tiny shambles of a ranch. Who had she been trying to fool, to think she could make a go of it all on her own? She felt the first hot sting of tears.

"Actually, I'm doing you a favor, Elsie. Now you can give up on this silly dream," Earl said. "You can go back home. You shouldn't be training horses with that leg of yours, anyway."

The tears dried before they even hit her cheeks and a scorching gust of anger blew through her chest. How dare he, she thought, act as if he knew what was best for her.

"Earl, you sneaky little cheat. You aren't doing me any favors! You are, as you always are, only looking out for yourself." She bent and picked up a handful of the very dirt Earl had so willingly sold out from underneath her, and hurled it right at his face and shiny car.

"You're crazy!" he said as he hurried to climb into his black SUV. "Be out of here by the first of the month. That's when they start digging."

He roared away, tires kicking up gravel around the curve in the road. Elsie walked over to her old horse, climbed up the corral fence, and then slipped her leg over his back. The two of them sat and watched the mustang and the sunset turn the world to gold, orange, and finally purple before shadows made it impossible to see the horizon. Only then did she let the fiery tears free. They scalded their way down her cheeks. She needed a new plan, fast.

Who could she call? Who would want a broke cowgirl with a limp and a couple of worthless horses? It wasn't like she had the money to put down on a ranch of her own. She felt like sitting in the dirt and feeling sorry for herself. She probably would've done just that but then the image of a long hospital corridor stretching out in front of her appeared in her mind's eye. If only she was cut from the same cloth as the rest of the women in her family. Somehow she had been born with a wild streak that etched its way through her soul, deeper and wider than any manmade canyon. She'd tried to explain to those around her that she just couldn't do the normal thing. Sometimes she wished she could, but it wasn't an option. Very slowly, she ran her hand over Sky's shoulder. The horse looked back, touching his nose to her boot. Elsie wasn't ready to give up. Her whole body resolute, she slid from the horse's broad back, picked up her lariat, and entered the round pen with the mustang. He eyed her from across the stretch of dust. She reached her hand out in a peaceful way. He lowered his head and charged right at her. Elsie ran, her boots kicking up trails of dust, though not as much as the thousand-pound animal behind her. Bravery returned once she had reached the safety of the corral rails. She turned, raised her arms and the rope, and scared the horse to a stop. The two looked at each other and it was hard to say who looked the more irritated with the other—horse or person. How was she ever going to ride this wild beast?

Another car pulled in off the road and Elise turned to see her mother's clean sedan park next to her horse trailer. In one night she was having more visitors than in the last two weeks put together.

"Elsie?" Lina Rosewood said.

"Hi, Mom," Elsie said.

"Are you okay? Earl called me and said he was worried that you were in over your head. Did you go buy a mustang?" Lina said.

"No, Mom. I didn't buy a mustang. I'm training one for a competition," Elsie said. "Earl only called you because he's selling the ranch and violating our lease agreement." She paused, hoping to garner a bit of her mother's sympathy. "With no notice."

Lina stood next to the corral, crossed her arms, and

looked at the horse standing with his head up and ears swiveling.

"Oh, Elsie," Lina said. She didn't say anything else but stood with her clean, pressed scrubs and perfect manicure. Lina was a surgery nurse who spent her days in the high-stress operating rooms helping to save the lives of numerous people. Elsie suspected her mother had no idea from where her youngest daughter's passionate, headstrong love affair with horses came.

Elsie climbed over the corral gate and stood next to her mother. "Please, Mom; don't say anything about my choices tonight. I'm pretty tired. I know you think I'm crazy, but I want this."

"Oh, Elsie. I know you do. I'm just a mother and so I worry," Lina said. She reached out and pulled her daughter to her. "How's your leg feeling? How about if you come to the house on Sunday?"

"Yes, Mom. I'm fine, don't worry! I'll come on Sunday, if I can."

"Okay," Lina said. She brushed her clothes off and got back in her vehicle. The night was clear and silent as the taillights faded into the growing dark. Elsie wished she was actually as confident as she had pretended to be around her mother.

***

Later, at the local bar, Elsie sat at a booth by herself, cradling a dollar beer special in both of her hands.

"Elsie?"

She looked up to see Rosa staring at her. Rosa had been roommates with her sister in college and then married a man from Montana.

"Hi, Rosa," Elsie said. "Is Landon back home visiting his grandmother?"

"Yes," Rosa replied. "She's strong and healthy as ever."

"Good. Have you been out to see my sister?"

"Yesterday. You look terrible. Were you sitting in the dust?"

"Thanks, I really needed to hear that tonight," Elsie said. She kept looking at her beer but felt herself begin to smile. Rosa's frankness had always been disarming.

"Sorry. What's wrong? Come on, it's Friday night and you're sitting here all alone. And dirty, really dirty. You're a pretty girl and you come to the bar looking like this?" Rosa said.

"Earl is selling the ranch I lease and I just brought home a wild mustang to train. The damn horse is crazy and mean. He tried to run me down today in the corral," Elsie said.

"Oh, I understand the dirt now," Rosa said. "But seriously, I'm sorry. You need a better ranch than that little ramshackle barn. You need a nice ranch. Maybe this is a blessing in disguise?"

"It's so well disguised that it feels like the end of the road. I swear I can feel my whole family just waiting for me to mess up so that I have to come crawling back to them and go to nursing school. It's like they don't even care that it would make me crazy."

"Let me ask my dear friend Lenora if you could go to Bear Dance Ranch," Rosa said. "It's in Montana, close to where we live. Maybe you could put on demonstrations for the guests. You know? Like how to break a wild horse?"

Elsie rested her head on her hands. "I can't do demonstrations with my wild horse. I can't even touch him. 'Oh, look, let's watch a stupid girl get herself killed,' people would say. It would be worse than a bear fight. Seriously, Rosa, I'm doomed."

"Stop feeling sorry for yourself! Gosh, to hear you talk! You have big dreams and the guts to try for them, so just quit being melodramatic. Let's come up with the next step," Rosa said.

Elsie sat up and looked at Rosa. Of course, the other woman was right, and it did burn a little to hear that she was being called out for feeling sorry for herself.

"Okay, thanks for asking Lenora," Elsie said. She could feel her cheeks and neck flushing. The beer must be filling her with self-pity, she thought, not courage.

Never one to wait, Rosa pulled out her cell phone and called Lenora. Landon, Rosa's very tall, very attractive husband came over from the bar with drinks and a basket of chips and pretzels.

"Hi, Elsie, have you eaten today?" Landon said.

"I don't know," Elsie replied. Her stomach had been in knots before she picked up her mustang.

"She's in a funk about the wild horse she just brought home to train. And now she just found out Earl is selling out to the fracking people. Thanks for the drinks," Rosa said. "I'm trying to get a hold of Lenora and see if they would let Elsie stay there."

Landon sat down and took off his hat. His eyes were deep blue and he had a tiny dark mole next to the laugh lines on the left side of his face. "They need help with the baby coming and all. I know Lenora needs hands in the kitchen. Can you cook, Elsie?" he said.

"Can she cook? Really, Landon? Thank God you're the sexiest man alive because you say the most ridiculous things sometimes. She wants to train horses, especially the wild and crazy kind, not cook dinner," Rosa said.

Landon laughed and winked at Elsie before giving his wife a swift kiss that made Elsie feel as if there was some sort of very personal secret between them.

That night in her tiny bed, Elsie listened to the coyotes howling and yipping and felt more lost than she had in a long time. After facing so many challenges, she wondered if her stubborn streak was the only thing which kept her chasing this dream of being a horse trainer. Some days, most days, it seemed like the whole world was stacked against her. She wondered if she should just quit now, before this whole crazy dream broke her heart in half as surely as it had broken her body.

As she drifted toward sleep, she saw Corbin Darkhorse, not the real-life, grown-up man from the stockyards, but rather the boy he had been. She felt the grip of his hand on her wrist as he pulled her up behind him on his horse. Her teenage-heart was thundering with the pulse of first love; it was as intoxicating as the rush of the galloping horse beneath them. He wrapped one arm around her, helping to steady her body against his and she gripped his waist. They raced out of the gate and toward the open prairie, their horse as excited as them to leave behind the confines of civilization. When they stopped next to a stand of cottonwoods lining the creek, Elsie slid from behind the saddle. Corbin grinned down at her then hooked his leg over the horn and dismounted facing her. He grabbed her by the waist and pulled her against him, bending his head to breathe and nibble along her neck. Her arms reflexively draped over his shoulders and she a tiny gasp of pleasure escape her lips as his tongue met her skin. A gust of hot prairie wind rustled the cottonwood leaves and Elsie breathed in the scent of Corbin's sweat-dampened skin. He pulled her into the shade of the trees, kissing her lips, cheeks, and forehead and then along her exposed shoulder and collarbone. He sat on the ground, holding her hand, smiling up at her with his black hair in his eyes. She knelt next to him, the ground steady beneath her knees. In one easy movement, he shifted her onto his lap, stroking his fingers through her hair. Their horse lipped at the grass along the creek bank and the sound of water running over river rocks filled the afternoon air. With his left hand, he pulled her toward him and she closed her eyes as his lips touched hers.

She rolled over in bed and smelled the sweet scent of wild sage coming through the half-open window of the horse trailer. The coyotes yipped again from the hill. She was awake as she felt the old anger course through her veins. Best to leave the good and bad memories alone, she

21

reasoned, because Corbin was not to be trusted.

***

The stars came out as Corbin unhooked the horse trailer. He rolled his shirt sleeves to his elbows to better feel the night breeze on his skin. Straightening up, he tried once again to focus his mind on the task at hand. He needed to make good time getting to the airport so that he could catch his flight to Kentucky, yet somehow he kept replaying over and over again the brief, disastrous encounter at the stockyards. Knowing he should be driving away from his brother's ranch, he reached inside the open truck window and shut off the diesel engine. A few steps from the truck and he was swallowed by the night. Darkness embraced him and he rolled his sleeves up even further. The way her body had stiffened at the sound of his voice kept haunting him. He ran his hand over his face and looked up at the stars. After spotting her, standing next to the rails looking in on that wild horse, he had wanted to step in and touch her shoulder. Somehow, he had convinced himself that when they finally met again, she would have heard of him, that she would be impressed by all he had accomplished so far in the horse world. What he really had hoped, had fooled himself into believing, was that she would see into his heart and know how sorry he truly was. How many times he'd wanted to go back and curse the young, scared boy he had been. He would have told his gangly-legged teenager self to be brave, to swallow the rising panic and stay in the hospital room. Running, as he now knew, eased nothing.

After ten years, he wished he had the right words in his mouth. When Elsie stiffened her shoulders and then turned to look at him, he felt her anger and resentment. Something quick and defensive had risen to the surface inside him and he'd spoken flippantly. His words were not the ones he'd imagined on countless sleepless nights.

Instead, fear for her jumped his heart rate up and adrenaline rushed through his blood, and he realized too late, even as the words left his mouth, that she would hear a challenge and not understand this was his sorry attempt at apologizing.

He wished she had read the letters he had sent. Only two, of course. He'd been defensive in the first. Apologizing in the beginning and then justifying his actions in the next sentence. It had been hard to admit to himself what a coward he had been. The second letter was better, more honest. He'd hoped she would respond. She had not.

Corbin ran his hand over his face. All he ever seemed to do with Elsie was make things worse. Perhaps, he thought, he would have another decade to try to figure out how to explain his sorry attempt at an apology at the stockyards.

CHAPTER TWO

"You can move to Bear Dance Ranch," Rosa said. "Lenora needs the help. Landon will be there in an hour to help you pack up the horses."

Elsie pulled the phone away from her ear for just a second and closed her eyes, relief flooding through her body. "Thank you so much," she said. She stood in the small barn with a wheelbarrow full of hay. Suddenly, the world didn't seem so mean and indifferent anymore.

Landon had a big truck and trailer which he backed right up to the mustang's pen. With a little encouragement, the horse jumped into the trailer and they closed the door behind him.

"What have you named him?" Landon asked.

"I think I might call him Magic," Elsie said.

"I have to say, he's a good-looking horse. I'm not much on those wild ones but he's a fine animal."

"Thanks, Landon. Thanks for everything, actually. Do you know Lenora and the Ranviers well?" Elsie said.

"They're a really great group of people," Landon replied. "Annie and Byron—they're getting up in age, but they still run that place pretty darn well. Lenora is actually their niece but they treat her like the daughter they never had. When she moved out to Montana a few years ago, she turned that place around and it's quite a guest ranch now. She married Clay last year. He's a good hand with a horse. The two of us used to rodeo some and run around together. In fact, he's one of the best men I know."

"I see." Elsie felt nervous as she thought about meeting the close-knit family. She had been living on her own for a long while and she felt a little rangy and unkempt like the coyotes in the hills.

"You'll get on just fine with that crew. Now let's go," Landon said. "Oh, I almost forgot, Clay's brother helps out from time to time. Not sure when you'll meet him. He's back east working with racehorses right now. Some sort of big-shot trainer." He shook his head and Elsie was unsure if he was annoyed with the brother or with the whole fashionableness of horse trainers that flew around the country. "Anyway, the two of you might work together some, doing demonstrations for the guests and such. Clay and I talked about some possibilities, but of course you'll have to work out the details."

Elsie pointed Sky toward the open trailer door and the beautiful chestnut stepped into the trailer of his own accord. Then she climbed into her own truck and slowly pulled out of the dirt drive, following behind Landon's rig. She looked in her rearview mirror as the tiny barn and dusty fields grew smaller and smaller. She would miss the place. It wasn't much of a ranch but it had been her first little home all her own.

Bear Dance Ranch was as different from the dusty place Elsie had just left as was possible. Mountains framed the ranch and meadows on three sides. A long stretch of river carved through the low pastures, enclosing the ranch on the fourth side. The buildings were well maintained with new roofs, and rows of flowers and bushes lined the paths and drives leading from the main ranch house to the many barns, arena, and guesthouses. Landon backed his trailer up to a corral behind the big barn. Together, he and Elsie coxed the mustang out into his new home.

"Pretty nice, isn't it?" Landon said.

"Yeah, it really is." Elsie could feel herself smiling.

"Come on, I'll take you in to meet everyone."

Elsie tried to smooth her long, brown hair into a controlled braid. What would they think of her, she wondered. She had scrubbed her face as clean as she could get it in her tiny shower yet her boots were nearly worn through and her best jeans were stained.

Landon and Elsie headed toward the ranch house. Halfway there, a couple appeared around the corner of the barn.

"Welcome!" the woman said. She had hair the color of Elsie's favorite chestnut pony growing up.

"Landon, thanks for bringing her over," the Lakota man said.

"Elsie, this is Clay and Lenora." Landon made introductions and then kissed Lenora on the cheek and hugged Clay.

Elsie smiled and shook hands. They looked like a couple out of a western magazine. Lenora was gorgeous and curvy and wore the most amazing green dress with beautiful bracelets on her slender wrists. Clay was Lakota and reminded her of someone, but her tired mind could not think of whom. He wore chaps with fringe over his work-roughened boots and a dark cowboy hat partially covered his black hair.

Elsie realized she was staring at the patch of skin where his shirt was unbuttoned and so she quickly said, "Thanks so much for taking me in. I really appreciate it."

"We're glad to have you. Helping the guests learn to ride can be tricky and we really need someone with horse experience and lots patience," Lenora said.

"I'm ready, I really am. I just needed a place for my horses and me to call home," Elsie said.

"We can't wait for you to meet Clay's brother. We

think the two of you could start doing demonstrations for the guests. We have even thought maybe clinics here at the ranch?" Lenora said.

"She just got here, Nora." Clay placed his hand on his wife's arm. "Lenora gets pretty excited about the ranch."

"Sorry, sorry. Please come in and have dinner and you can get some good rest tonight. We can figure everything out in the morning," Lenora said.

"Come on in for dinner, Landon." Clay smiled at his friend. "Lenora made that apple crisp for dessert, you know, the one you loved last fall?"

"Well, you had me at, 'Lenora made.' Let me call Rosa and see if she wants to come out too. She won't like it if I eat apple crisp without her," Landon said.

Everyone walked to the ranch house. Along the way, Clay and Lenora pointed out the huge riding arena, the cow barn, and the two horse barns. Tucked away from the main ranch were the guest cabins, which were converted ranch hand quarters but now dripped of rustic-Montana-luxury.

"Clay's brother stays out there in the old bunkhouse, where Clay used to live before we got married," Lenora said. She pointed out a weathered building attached to the main horse barn.

If Clay's brother was half as good-looking as Clay, Elsie suspected the female guests would really like those horse-training demonstrations. She just hoped whoever this guy was he was not one of those full-of-himself horse trainer types.

The ranch house was large and open. Aged-pine floorboards creaked under Elsie's feet and she admired the massive beams spanning the ceiling. Hand-woven rugs warmed the living and dining area and two floor-to-ceiling windows showcased the pastures and mountains to the west.

"Byron, Annie, she's here!" Lenora called up the stairs.

Elsie tucked her hair behind her ears and tried to look

more confident than she felt.

Annie was small and compact. Her smile helped Elsie ease the tension she felt building between her shoulder blades. Byron took off his reading glasses as he came down the stairs. "You're training a mustang, I hear?" he said.

"Yes," Elsie replied.

Byron looked steadily at Elsie and she squared her shoulders and met his eyes.

"Good," Byron said. "We have a ranch full of strong women and I think you'll fit right in."

Elsie felt a huge smile pull the corners of her lips up. She was a strong woman, she realized, even if she did not always feel that way.

There was a knock at the door and Rosa appeared. She kissed Landon and hugged Lenora before putting her arm around Elsie's waist. "I told you you'd like it here."

"Thanks," Elsie whispered. "Really, thank you."

***

Dinner was delicious and loud. Elsie found herself eating and listening to the story of how Lenora and Clay had ended up together.

"Almost a whole year and these two ignored each other," Annie said, nodding at Clay and Lenora. "Even though sparks flew so thick and fast that you could barely see anytime the two were even in the same room together."

"Yes, well," Clay said. "She was hard to convince, that's all."

"You were just like your little brother is now," Lenora said. "You had women lined up to see you and I wanted no part of that."

"That's before I saw you, Nora. You know I wanted you, and only you from then on," Clay spoke slowly. "Plus, she makes it out like there were all these women. But really the only women who wanted me were looking for a crash-test dummy to ride their fancy colts."

"Speaking of that brother of yours, when is he coming back from Lexington?" Rosa said.

"He was supposed to yesterday, but then he called and said he had this other plan. Who knows what that means with my brother." Clay waved his fork in exasperation.

"I bet he's met a southern belle, and that's what's keeping him," Landon said.

"Just one? That boy probably has ten girls waiting for him." Rosa snorted.

There was more laughter and another bottle of wine was opened. Elsie was dreading working with the younger brother before she had even met him. There was nothing she hated more than a guy who thought he was God's gift to women—plural. Well, the only thing she hated more than that was a guy who thought he knew how to train horses better than she. Just because the horse world tended to appreciate male horse trainers more than females did not mean that Elsie wasn't as good as all the guys with their boots and hats and custom spurs. Hopefully, she could do whatever little demonstration was expected of her with this guy and then train her mustang in peace. She reminded herself that this was only temporary until she could win the competition and put a down payment on a ranch of her own.

"Who's ready for dessert?" Lenora said.

Elsie smiled and tried to be polite and not dwell on her misgivings about any future demonstrations with the elusive brother.

"Have you named that wild mustang of yours yet, Elsie?" Clay said.

"I think I'll call him Magic," Elsie said. She didn't tell them she hoped the horse would put a little magic into her last-chance career.

***

The sun was just sending probes of easterly light over the peaks as Elsie stepped into the chill air. She pulled a loose wrap around her body. The morning was still cool and fresh and she knew she would be alone for a half hour or so.

The mustang watched her from across the corral. She whistled for Sky and her reining horse came trotting out of the morning mist. She let him lip the carrot piece from her palm and then she grabbed a fistful of his mane and swung up in a graceful bound to land on his broad back. Without bridle or saddle, she directed her horse to the gate of the mustang's pen, opened it from horseback, and then shut it again once they were inside.

The mustang raised his head, his nostrils flared and eyes wary as he watched Elsie and her horse approach. They stopped; the mustang stood, pawed the ground but kept his eyes on them. Elsie pulled her wrap free from her shoulders and let it rest on the withers of her horse. She sat in the early morning light, in nothing but a tank top, which had a bit of frayed lace around the bodice, and pale-pink panties. Her bare toes wiggled as she delighted in being bareback and barefoot on her horse at the start of such a beautiful day. She urged Sky forward into a slow canter. The two moved together effortlessly. Elsie's long brown hair blew out behind her and she closed her eyes, letting her mind relax into the flow of movement. She shifted her weight and brought her horse down to a stop, then spun him quickly to change directions. She moved toward the mustang, pushing him with her own horse, encouraging him to join them and to run with their small herd. He spooked, snorted, and then reluctantly began to canter with them. Elsie urged him forward until he was beside her own horse by shaking her wrap.

The mustang and her own horse became a unit: cantering, communicating by body language, flowing together. She felt a grin creeping up on her face and she let it come. This was going to work, she realized, she could train this wild horse if she just used her heart and gut and let the rest fall into place. Finally, she slowed her horse, letting the mustang slow too and then the three of them stood and breathed in the cool morning air. Elsie smiled broadly, her body tingling and alive with the joy of being one with these amazing creatures.

Suddenly, she looked up. They were not alone. A man stood next to her trailer. For a second, she thought it was Clay but realized this man was too young. She pulled her wrap over her exposed legs and felt a bolt of anger course through her veins. Great, she thought, nice home she had complete with a Peeping Tom already set to watch her private rides in the morning.

"You could've called out you were there." Elsie raised her voice and spoke to the man.

She rode her horse over to the corral. No reason for her to be shy now, she thought. Who knew how long he'd been watching. She had better face this head on.

The man stepped away from the trailer and the fresh morning light caught in his pure black hair. Corbin Darkhorse stood before her. She tried not to gasp.

"I didn't want to break the spell." Corbin spoke very carefully. "Imagine my surprise, to come home and find Elsie Rosewood riding naked in the morning sun."

"I was not naked, and it was a private, morning ride with my horses. I would appreciate you not sneaking up on me again," Elsie said.

He stepped up to the round pen fence and smiled. The sun caught his black hair and his eyes were huge and dark, and teeth bright white in the morning light. The top two buttons of his shirt were undone. He rolled up his sleeves to reveal more beautiful skin both rich and dark. Elsie remembered, all too well, running her fingers over it. She hated herself for noticing him in such an intimate way.

"I was hardly sneaking," he said. "*Transfixed*, might be a better word. Actually, I was wondering why you're at my brother's ranch."

"I live here now," Elsie answered. "I'm going to do clinics for the guests while I train my mustang."

Of course, she realized, Clay looked a lot like Corbin. She had been so tired, so frustrated and worried that her brain had tried to warn her yesterday and she had ignored the signs. The offer to come and live at Bear Dance Ranch had seemed like the most serendipitous gift and had restored some of her faith in her chosen career path. Now the cost seemed too high. After such a long span of time, why was Corbin reappearing in all aspects of her life?

"I brought home a mustang too, nice big-boned gray beast. Got a halter on him but that's about it." He rested his arms on the top rail of the round pen and looked up at Elsie sitting on her horse. "I'm calling him 'Second Chance.'"

Pure anger shot through her. How dare this arrogant man, who obviously didn't have to convince anyone in the world that *he* should train horses, bring back a horse for the competition she had to win. He would be the favorite; the famous Corbin Darkhorse with his little horse-training quips and poetic sayings. Biting her lip so hard she thought she could taste blood, she turned back to look at her mustang. Magic watched her from the far side of the pen, ears moving as he assessed the whole situation.

"Good luck to you," Elsie said. She spoke while still watching her mustang. She couldn't even look at Corbin. "I suppose you're the infamous little brother?"

"Yes, I am. But don't believe all the stories they tell out here at Bear Dance Ranch," he said. "Most of them Clay makes up for fun."

Elsie turned away from her mustang and forced herself to look right at him. He was smiling as if he had a secret and did not want her to know what it was. She remembered she was still wearing only underwear and a thin shirt. Quickly, she looked down and realized that both of her nipples could be seen through the white fabric.

He was looking at her tits, she thought in a rush of

anger.

"God, you seriously have no class at all," Elsie said. "And I already know it's not going to work for us to do riding demonstrations together. This was a bad idea to come here."

She turned her horse with her legs and trotted off to the corral gate.

"Don't get so uptight," he replied. "You were the one who decided to ride your horse *half-naked*, at the ranch where *I* live."

There was no point, she decided, in even dignifying his statement with her view on the situation. She had lived by herself for the past couple of years and was used to being able to ride her horses whenever and however she wanted. She was also used to being surrounded by quiet and there was nothing she hated more than a man with a big opinion of himself. Corbin definitely fit that bill, and he probably thought he was doing her a favor by staring at her chest.

She slipped down from her horse, pulled her wrap around her waist like a skirt, and walked out of the corral. Inside her trailer, she dressed quickly in jeans and a bra and a long-sleeve shirt, and then hurried to the ranch house. There was no point in trying to stay at Bear Dance. Lenora and Clay and everyone else seemed just great, but there was no way she would be able to work with the most challenging horse of her life while dealing with this annoying, arrogant, womanizing, sexy—where had that last thought come from?—man.

Halfway to the ranch, she was met by both Clay and Lenora.

"Morning. How'd you sleep?" Lenora asked.

"Listen, thanks so much for offering me the chance to stay," Elsie said. "But I don't think it's going to work out."

"Why not?" Clay said.

"Because she's all worked up about me looking at her boobs," Corbin said.

She had not realized he was following her.

"What the hell, Corbin?" Lenora and Clay said at the same time.

"It's not my fault. I pull up after a long night of driving and find Elsie out riding her horse without any tack—or much in the way of clothing," Corbin said. "I had no idea she was going to get so worked up about it."

"Wow, I'm really sorry," Clay said. "Please stay. He will be on his best behavior from now on, I'm sure of it."

"Look, it's not that big of a deal," Elsie said. She was trying to keep her voice calm and face free of any emotion. "It's just that I'm not sure this is the right fit for me. I'm used to working on my own with the horses and I just don't know how this place will fit into my training needs."

"Elsie," Corbin said. "It's not like we're strangers. I've seen you naked before, a long time ago to be fair, but I still think you're blowing this out of proportion."

"Out of proportion?" Elsie felt her fists ball at her sides. She knew she was leaning toward Corbin, her face tightening. All she wanted was to grab him by the throat and shake him until that smile was gone from his beautiful lips. This was the man who had walked out when she needed him most.

"We dated one summer on the circuit," Corbin said in answer to Clay's and Lenora's questioning looks.

"It ended badly between you two." Clay stated the obvious. He was giving his younger brother a hard stare.

Elsie wanted to be back on her horse. The morning had started so well, and she could still feel the uncomplicated joy of running with her small herd.

"We dated." She spoke almost to herself. The casualness of his words stung. She looked away at the mountains.

"Elsie, I didn't mean it like that." He almost sounded like he was pleading with her. She would've liked to look at his face and read his eyes but her own were dangerously close to tears. She pinched the inside of her palm hard enough to sting. All she had to do was pull her anger around her; it settled over her shoulders with the ease of an old ally, its strength inflexible and cold. She turned and walked away from the small group. It was time to leave.

"Elsie," Lenora called. She sounded desperate. "We need you. Please stay, we will try to give you as much privacy as we can. What a great way for you to start getting your name out by teaching the guests all about what you do with the horses?"

"Come on up and let's all have breakfast and you can think it over? Lenora made her famous blueberry muffins," Clay said.

"They are really good," Corbin interjected. Then low, so that only she could hear, he said, "I promise I've changed from the kid you knew before."

Elsie looked at him in disbelief. Her anger was firmly back in place and the softness of tears gone.

"Corbin, shut up," Clay said.

Elsie looked out over the meadows and then up to Bear Peak. She realized she wanted to train her mustang more than anything else in the world. The truth was she was out of options. There was nowhere else she could go and be able to train in relative peace. Perhaps, she could ignore Corbin and just train her horse. At least, she reasoned, she was no longer attracted to the arrogant fool. What could she do but stay? Stay and keep her shield up, her anger on and her heart focused on beating anyone who stood in her path to success.

CHAPTER THREE

The late afternoon sun was hot on Corbin's shoulders as he carried his gear over to where the gray mustang was penned. The big horse watched his approach with apprehension. The mustang kept his head raised and nostrils flared as he took in Corbin's scent and studied the man holding a bundle of tack. Corbin knew the horse saw him as one and the same with the captors who had rudely gathered the animal from his life of freedom running the steppes. He rested the saddle over the rail of the pen and then climbed up to perch on the top. "You're not the only one who is less than happy to see me today." The horse didn't seem impressed with his self-pitying statement. He imagined that his mustang was talking to the black one corralled on the other side of the ranch. He could not help but wonder if his brother had intentionally not told Elsie that she wasn't the only competitor with a mustang at the ranch. Clay had always been one to look out for his younger brother and Corbin appreciated it, he really did, but it seemed that close proximity was not the best way to fix the wrong he had done to Elsie all those years ago. In fact, after his performance at the stockyards, he really had not been looking forward to seeing her again so quickly.

He needed time to sort out how he would apologize and win her over. He chalked that one up to his own thick-skulled inability to seem to really learn the lessons life kept throwing at him. With time, he had hoped, the right words would come to him in a better circumstance, but somehow he kept getting thrown in with her at the wrong time and saying the wrong thing.

The horse snorted and looked at him with disgust. Not for the first time, Corbin wondered exactly how much the four-legged creatures could read human minds. When he had pulled in with his truck that morning and saw an old beat-up horse trailer sitting behind the old cow barn, he had thought it looked a lot like Elsie Rosewood's trailer. He could remember very clearly how it had looked pulling out of the stockyards as he cursed himself for being so cocky and for letting his fear to see Elsie get hurt again influence his choice of words. Elsie had always been proud. So incredibly fierce and independent, and he quickly realized she had not softened with time nor had she forgiven him for his abrupt departure from her life. Not that he blamed her. He had not forgiven himself.

To be fair, he had tried to apologize in the awkward, long, and somewhat confusing, letters he had sent. He imagined she had read them but he was also realistic enough to know that she might have tossed them in the trash basket without even tearing open the envelopes.

Apologies were never good. Better to not be in the position of needing to give an apology in the first place. He knew a lot about being on the receiving end of admissions of guilt and wrong. "Sorry for missing your birthday, Son." That had been a favorite of his father. And of course he could not forgive the "Sorry, forgot to come get you for the ball game, the rodeo, that movie with the cowboy." The list was long. Corbin watched the gray horse sniff the saddle blanket. One delicate ear kept tabs on Corbin. He didn't move but instead let the horse investigate on his own terms. "Did you know your dad?"

At the sound of his voice, the horse glanced at him and took two fast steps backward. "Sore subject?" Corbin thought the horse looked as if he wished the annoying human would just go away. "No can-do, buddy. We're in this thing together." He jumped from his perch on the rails, down into the pen, and started swinging his rope to get the horse trotting in big circles around him. Somehow, he would have to show her that he was sorry. Somehow, he would have to prove to Elsie that he had changed and the past was not the future.

***

Lenora came around the corral where Elsie was grooming Sky. The chestnut-haired woman had two glasses of lemonade with mint sprigs wedged between the ice cubes. Elsie was quickly realizing that Lenora wanted to feed any and everyone. She stifled the ungracious thought before it could devolve further. It had been a long time since people had been so kind to her and she knew she was judging Lenora on her past experiences and not on the woman's current actions.

Lenora set the glasses down next to the round pen and let Sky sniff her fingers. "He's a good-looking boy."

"Thanks, the very first horse I trained for reining competitions."

"I bet it feels weird to be at a small guest ranch away from all the excitement?"

Elsie took a deep breath and looked out over the meadow leading down to the river and the blue sky with a few loose clouds scatted across the expanse. "I think I need a place to incubate this new project with my mustang. I'm very grateful you've let me stay here."

"The timing is perfect, actually," Lenora said. "Can I show you around a little and get you oriented for the guests that arrive later today?"

"Yes, thank you. I'm not afraid of hard work and I can

help out with anything that needs to be done. I'm just letting you know I'm not very good in the kitchen. Well, actually, I'm terrible in the kitchen, but I can do about anything on the ranch or with a horse."

Lenora laughed. "I love how earnest you are! Don't worry. I'm pregnant but not bedridden, so you won't be left alone in a kitchen anytime soon!"

Elsie's first week at Bear Dance Ranch was full of teaching guests to ride horses and training her mustang. After a few days, she was able to walk up to Magic and put a halter on his head, and then lead him around the pen. It was hard, but she tried to not watch Corbin train his own mustang. He was already teaching the big gray horse to wear a saddle and bridle. But she knew that Magic was not a horse she could quickly push toward trust. Not only was he wild, but he also seemed to distrust humans and the new world around him more than Corbin's gray.

Elsie did most of her training in the early mornings when the ranch was still filled with the peace of night and seemed to be all hers. The horses were awake, as were the red-winged blackbirds, which nested in the cattails fringing the tiny stock pond next to her trailer. As soon as she woke, Elsie would get fully dressed, in case Corbin decided to pay her a surprise visit, and go out to the corral where her mustang lived. Magic watched her from the opposite end of the pen as she sat down on an upturned bucket and closed her eyes. In her mind, she pictured the black horse approaching her, his head down and eyes soft with curiosity and gentleness. She would reach her hand out and brush her fingers through his thick mane and work out the snarls from running in the wind. In her mind, she would grab a fistful of his mane and swing herself up onto his broad back. She could feel the muscles play under her thighs, then the two of them would be off like the Montana wind, rushing, roaring, galloping.

She opened her eyes and found the mustang a few feet away, watching her. His eyes were dark as pools of still water. Very slowly, he took two more steps toward her. She closed her eyes. Magic blew softly through his nose, ruffling Elsie's hair; he brushed his lips across her head. Her heart beat with such joy; this huge wild animal was starting to trust her. She reached her hand up and scratched under his jaw, just behind the soft protrusion of his lower lip. Magic closed his eyes, letting her run her fingers along his neck and then up to the spot on his withers where horses loved to groom each other. Slowly, she stood, keeping her body movements controlled. The mustang opened his eyes but didn't shy away from her. She kept scratching his withers and soon he lowered his head and half closed his eyes again.

"Are you planning on riding that horse?" She heard from behind her. Magic startled and raised his head.

Elsie turned and found Corbin grinning at her. "You know that's part of the competition, right? Riding the horses and all?"

"Stop scaring my horse." Her tone was less than inviting.

"You can't train a horse in a bubble, Elsie," he said. "There's going to be noise and people and sounds at the competition."

"How about you don't talk to me unless it's about the riding demonstration we have to do together, okay?" Elsie said. "That way I don't have to think about a thousand different ways I would like to cut out your tongue with my very dull spur."

"Geeze, a little grouchy this morning?" Corbin was still smiling.

"I assume you're here because you want to practice our demonstration for the guests?" Elsie said. She brushed her hand over Magic's shoulders and back and then turned away from the wild horse and faced Corbin.

He was wearing an old shirt with the sleeves rolled up and broken-in cowboy boots. His dark hair was still wet from a shower and his eyes were so intense she had to look away. She swallowed and made herself remember his annoying comment just moments earlier.

Corbin opened the stock gate for her and she walked out of the pen. She could smell the scent of pines trees and wild sage as she passed close by his body.

"You are grouchy this morning," he stated. "I thought you loved mornings."

"I do. You just annoy me." This was true, but oh how thankful she was, that annoyance had replaced the hurt. She kept walking ahead of Corbin, hoping he would stop speaking. When they reached the horse pasture, she whistled for Sky. Her beautiful horse raised his head and cantered over to the gate.

"You know, Elsie. I've been called a lot of things by a lot of girls but 'annoying' isn't one of them," Corbin said. "Maybe we could go for a ride, just you and me?"

Elsie put the halter on Copper Sky and led him through the gate. Corbin caught his horse, Nighthawk, and the four of them headed to the barn in silence.

Halfway up the hill, Elsie said, "Maybe, Corbin, the problem isn't with me. Just maybe, all those girls that you so fondly remember are too silly to see what a conceited, full-of-himself man you really are?"

She heard laughter behind her.

"Maybe you're right. But one thing is for sure, Elsie." He paused for effect and she knew he was enjoying himself. "I still get under your skin."

Elsie bit the inside of her cheek. She had forgotten about his sense of humor. He was right, though she was not going to let him know how accurate his words really were. She stopped her horse and turned to him. His eyes were alive with laughter and a smile danced across his full lips.

"Let's just work on this performance thing and not talk about anything else. Okay?" Elsie said.

"Fine. Just trying to pass the time. You know, some people like to get to know the person they are going to be working with."

"I know all about you," she replied. "Remember?"

"Elsie, I do remember. But the thing is, I'm not that kid anymore. You and I need to take a ride together. Just us and the horses and the wind and sky."

She knew he wanted her to look up. Instead, she stared at the ground. Her throat felt too dry and her palms had grown damp. He said nothing else, so they saddled their horses in complete silence. Once in the big arena, they trotted circles and stretched out their horses' backs until the animals felt strong and sure. On a horse, Elsie felt so alive her whole body tingled. Her mind slowed down and her thoughts were purely in the moment. Minimal adjustments—a slight pressure with her calf or lifting of her diaphragm could bring her thousand-pound horse to a sliding stop or into a full gallop, depending upon the cue. Riding, no, horses, were what had kept her working during all the long hours of physical therapy after each surgery. She had needed something to live for because even though the doctors said she would never ride, let alone train horses again, she had been determined. At night, alone, the whole world had seemed against her. She would close her eyes and remember the feel of a living, breathing creature beneath her. The power and connection were too potent a draw for her to ever give up the dream of riding again.

Corbin was the first to stop in the middle of the arena. Elsie followed him a few minutes later.

"So what kind of tricks can you do?" Corbin asked.

In answer, Elsie leaned forward and removed her horse's bridle and let it fall to the ground. She urged Sky first into a full-shouldered gallop and then slid him into a perfectly executed stop. She cantered the other direction, showing her flying changes of lead at the center of the arena. Sky halted and this time she nudged his shoulder with the toe of her boot. He calmly went down on one knee and horse and rider bowed together.

"That's very good," Corbin said. Elsie thought she saw

some small glint of admiration in his eyes.

"So what about you?" She was curious to see if he was doing anything avant-garde with his horses.

In one fluid movement, Corbin flipped his leg over his horse's back so that he was riding backward. Horse and rider began canter a large circle. Corbin, while still riding backward, undid his lariat and began a large loop. As Nighthawk neared the fence post on the long side of the arena, Corbin swung the rope and neatly caught the post. His horse slid to a stop and backed up until Corbin could free his rope.

Once they were both in the center of the arena again, Elsie said, "Okay, so we both have some good skills. Now how do we incorporate them to make an entertaining show?"

"I have an idea," Corbin said. Carefully, he outlined a small performance.

They spent the rest of the time organizing each movement to best highlight their personal strength and those of their horses. When Corbin was not being flirtatious or annoying, Elsie thought she actually could stand to work with him. He was better with a horse than the boy she had known years ago. He seemed less hungry, surer of himself. The kid she'd known had been so ambitious, but it seemed Corbin had toned that down.

Elsie looked up from patting Sky's damp shoulder and saw Byron Ranvier watching them. The patriarch of Bear Dance Ranch wore a broad felt hat and a neatly buttoned and ironed shirt.

"Looks pretty good," Byron called. He leaned both hands against the rail of the arena as he watched the riders.

Corbin and Elsie walked their tired horses over to the fence. Byron pushed his hat back on his head and looked up at the riders. "No more problems between the two of you."

Byron was not asking a question. Elsie looked at Corbin.

"No, sir," Corbin answered.

"Good. You two work well together so best to put any past differences aside and keep that in mind." Byron smoothed Sky's forelock out of his eyes.

"I keep telling her that," Corbin said. His tone was joking and he winked at Byron.

Elsie felt her shoulders tighten. "The past is in the past. But I've learned my lesson and I'll never trust Corbin again." She cued Sky forward and trotted toward the barn.

"Wait. Elsie, wait," Corbin said.

She did not turn around even when she heard the sound of his horse's hooves on the hard-packed dirt behind her. She slid from Sky and started loosening the cinch. He was directly behind her and she could smell pine and honey and the fresh-cut alfalfa they had raked that morning. Her nostrils flared with his scent and her arms came alive with feeling as he reached around her to still her hands. The usual urge to fight him, to push against his attempts to make up and tease her, died down. Her breathing became shallow as she let him almost hold her. When he spoke, his voice was so low and his lips were so close to her ear. "If I could go back and tell that silly boy I used to be..." He paused, his breath moving the stray hairs along the nape of her neck. "If I could tell him that he was making the worst decision of his life, I would."

The old anger came rushing back and her words were alive with the pain of the past. "Just say you're sorry!" She jerked away from the circle his arms had formed around her and faced him. For a brief moment, her anger wavered as she saw that his eyes were dark with something akin to sorrow. Maybe, she thought, he was really repentant? They stood close, facing each other, and for too long she stared into his eyes. Where was her anger, she wondered. She needed it now. This vulnerable feeling was uncomfortable and left her palms damp with uncertainty. "Don't try and make excuses or turn this into a poem about regret."

Nighthawk sneezed and blew the way horses do when

they're bored and Corbin looked down. "All right, Elsie. I'll be the asshole-cowboy. You can run around on your high horse. I deserve that."

He turned and walked away and Elsie watched him go. His broad shoulders squared and his horse easy by his side. For the space of time it took for Sky to nibble a few shoots of grass growing in the gravel at their feet, she thought about running after him. The urge passed and she unsaddled her horse.

***

Elsie was nearly asleep in her horse trailer when she smelled the very faint, but unmistakable, scent of fire. Her leg and hip ached a little from the extra exertion of training for the demonstration. She probably should not have tried to show off so much in front of Corbin, but he had made her so angry and she also wanted him to know that she was doing just fine without him. Performing to her best seemed the best way to illustrate this truth.

Slowly, she rolled over in bed. The sheets smelled like the fresh sprigs of lavender Lenora had given her to keep in the sleeping compartment of her trailer, but there was, unmistakably, a strong smell of smoke in the air. After so many years of living on ranches, she could not help herself, and so she got up to investigate.

Outside, the stars were bright and the air cool on her bare feet. She reached back in for her boots, slipped them on without socks, and very quietly walked toward the big barns and the smell of smoke. The far hay barn, with its dark doors flung open as the hay dried, glowed orange. Her heart jumped forward into a gallop. Without thinking, she ran for the hose attached to water hydrant close to the hitching rails. She unrolled it as fast as she could and headed toward the barn. As she ran she began to yell, "Fire!"

Thicker smoke met her at the entrance and she

46

stumbled over already burned ground outside the barn. The hose shot forth a thick stream of water and Elsie was relieved when she heard the ranch dogs begin to bark and knew that people would soon find her.

The smoke only thickened as she sprayed water into the smoky interior. She had no idea how the fire had started outside the barn, but she did know if it reached the stack of fresh hay, the whole barn would surely burn to the ground. Elsie heard footsteps behind her and she took a quick relieved breath; Corbin was followed by Clay, Annie, and Byron.

"Grab more hoses," Clay called out.

Elsie saw guests coming from their cabins and then saw Lenora urging then away from the fire. Corbin and Clay both hooked up hoses and began spraying the outside of the barn and also through one of the windows. Byron started the tractor and with Annie's help, they began to dig a fire ring around the back side of the barn. After a nerve-racking stretch of time, the flames began to diminish and the thick smoke thinned out. Corbin peeked in the entrance of the barn. "The fire didn't reach the new alfalfa," he called as he glanced back at the ring of worried people behind him. "It just burned the smaller stack of last season's hay."

Elsie took a deep breath and sank down to the ground, her legs suddenly so tired they would no longer hold her.

"Thank goodness," Annie said. "We would have lost the barn for sure had it made it to the fresh hay."

"Yes, thank goodness." Lenora came forward and knelt next to Elsie.

"How did you see it?" Corbin spoke as he turned away from the barn and also came to kneel next to Elsie.

"I smelled it when I was in bed." Her tongue felt gritty and thick with the smoke and ash.

"Thank you." Byron had gotten off the tractor and strode over to them. "You saved us."

"Elsie, we are so glad you came to Bear Dance." Clay

was grinning just like his brother as the stillness of night began to settle back over the ranch.

"Why was the ground burned outside the barn?" Elsie said.

"There must have been some mischief tonight." Byron looked back at the crowd of guests.

Annie rested her hand on his arm.

"I'll go find out," Lenora said. Clay wrapped his arm around his wife's waist and together they walked toward the guests.

"Thank you, Elsie." Annie's voice was full of warmth and she squeezed the younger woman's arm. "Let's go back to the ranch house and have something cool to drink.

"That's a great idea," Byron said as he led the way back up the slight hill.

"Are you okay?" Corbin said. He spoke in that low intimate way that reminded Elsie of the all-night conversations they used to have.

"Yes, I'm fine." She knew she was being brusque, but right now, she wanted a drink of water and a shower and then to sleep.

Inside the ranch kitchen, Annie doled out glasses of lemonade and then Byron proposed a toast. "To our newest member of Bear Dance Ranch, Elsie, you saved the day."

Elsie blushed and drank the cool and slightly sweet beverage. Clay and Lenora came into the kitchen with two teenage boys in tow and a very angry adult. Both boys apologized with downcast eyes as they explained how they tried to light a fire outside the barn and then left it when their parents called them inside. When nudged a little further by their father, they also admitted they lit the fire to hide the smell of the illicit cigarettes they were smoking. Elise felt herself smiling as she watched the two boys wriggle under the angry eyes of their Byron, Clay, and their father. A long silence stretched and the younger of the two boys started to cry, and Annie handed them glasses of lemonade as well. After a little pause, everyone, even Byron, was appeased by their apology and the promise to help the next day with the process of sorting the good hay bales form those which had been ruined by the smoke and fire.

CHAPTER FOUR

Outside of the round pen for only the second time, Elsie held the long rope attached to the Magic's halter. His ears were on her and though his eyes still had the wary look of a wild animal, she also saw a shadow of curiosity. Slowly, the fear this horse had felt was being replaced with interest. She couldn't help but smile as she directed the horse out on the line and he cooperated, moving into a slow trot. She asked Magic to change directions several times and watched with joy as the ear closest to her stayed locked onto her subtle body cues. She asked for a *whoa* and stopped her own body and then turned away from the horse. She waited, her back toward the mustang. Finally, she felt the tentative touch of a velvet nose on her shoulder. She turned and touched the horse's soft cheek and pulled his long forelock away from his eyes. Fishing in her pocket, she brought forth a nub of carrot and offered it to the soft lips. Magic carefully took the treat as Elsie bent and breathed in the scent of his wild mane. She could smell the pine forests cloaking the mountains to the west and the scent of alfalfa in his black hair. Warm sunshine made her shoulders relax, and for the first time in a long while, Elsie actually felt at peace with the world around her. She ran her hands down the mustang's neck and over his back. Magic kept his head low and his ears were listening to her and softly alert. She realized the mustang was starting to see her as part of his herd, and even more importantly, he was beginning to feel that she could keep him safe. She let him sniff along her thigh and hip; she had noticed that since her accident horses were curious about her leg. "That was a long time ago," she whispered as much to herself as to the wild horse.

A droning noise off to the east shook Elsie out of her quiet reverie and made her look up. She saw a small aircraft, low in the sky, heading toward the ranch. A bolt of fear shot through her: all of the mustangs were rounded up from the ranges with helicopters. The sound in the sky might take Magic back to the terrible day when he was driven from freedom, the last day he ever saw his family.

Elsie knew it was too late to try to make a dash for the round corral. She would have to stay calm and somehow keep her mustang under control as well. Already his head was raised and his ears were back as he heard the noise in the sky. She touched his neck, feeling the muscles coiled under her hands and ready to explode. She made a decision: she would send the mustang back out on the line and let him move his feet, and hopefully, this would keep him from feeling trapped. Elsie knew that if he tried to run, she would not be able to hold him. Her only chance to keep control of the situation was to try to use the training that Magic already understood to keep him calm.

The horrible drone of the small plane was close—right overhead. The thing was ridiculously low. Elsie glanced up to see a small, yellow body and brightly striped wings. She urged the mustang out and cued him to move his feet. His ears were flat back against his head and she watched in dismay as his eyes lost all of their soft curiosity. She could see pure, instinctual terror fill his body.

The mustang pulled hard on the rope and then reared, spinning on his haunches. Elise hung on, digging her boot heels into the soft dirt. The plane was right above Elsie and the mustang. She would've tried to speak to him, to calm him down, but all her energy was funneled into trying to hold the rope as Magic struggled for his freedom. The horse watched her, his eyes large with fear and then she saw him make the decision to rear again and spin. She had no chance to hold him as he threw his thousand pounds of muscle away from her.

The rope jerked, pulling Elsie off her feet. As her body hit the ground, she struggled to keep her grip on the line but it shot through her hands. The horse ran, as if his life depended upon it, up into the meadow below Bear Peak and then further. She could only hope that a fence stopped her horse before he made it all the way into the mountains.

"Stupid plane," she said. Her hands were bloody from the rope and she tasted tears and dust. The plane was gone, leaving behind the faint smell of exhaust.

"Come on. We'll go get him!" She heard from behind her. Sitting up, she saw Corbin on his black gelding, Nighthawk, cantering toward her.

She stood; he grabbed her hand and helped her swing up behind him. She clutched him around the waist and hung on as his horse gathered its haunches and sprung into a full gallop. They tore out of the pasture gate and up toward Bear Peak and the mustang. The wind whipped tears from Elsie's eyes as she tried to follow the plume of dust Magic kicked up in his headlong flight.

Halfway up, Corbin slowed Nighthawk. They walked, letting the horse breathe and blow.

"Are your hands okay?" Corbin said.

"I think so," Elsie replied.

"That damn pilot. I don't know what he thinks he's doing flying so low over our ranch." Corbin nearly spat the words.

"You don't have to do this," Elsie said. "It's my stupid mess anyway."

"There's a lot of land up here. I think you'll need some

help."

"Seriously, I can do it."

Corbin looked mad. She saw him glance off to the right and into the valley below them before answering.

"You need help," he stated. "Quit being so stubborn for just a minute, okay? You're a good horsewoman but you've got to quit being so hard-headed."

Maybe the note of sincerity in his voice, or maybe the hard fall earlier, made her bite back her first response, which was to tell him to go to hell. Instead, she was quiet, mulling over his words.

Finally, she said, "Has anyone ever told you that you can't be a horse trainer because you're a man? Or that you should give up on your dreams because they seem too big?"

"No." He glanced over his shoulder at her, his eyebrows drawn together like the angled wings of a hawk.

"Everyone tells me, all the time, how I can't succeed in this business," Elsie said. "Everyone thinks I'm crazy for wanting to gentle this mustang. Corbin, do you know how that feels? Do you? They say those things because I'm a girl."

She could feel the sting of tears, just a blink away, and so she bit the inside of her cheek hard.

"Maybe they don't want to see you get hurt again?" He paused, his words careful. "I'm sorry. I never thought how hard it might be for you."

"Of course not. No guy ever does. But they like to make sure it's next to impossible for a girl to get into their horse training club. You know what? All those nos. All that, you-can't-do-that-little-girl stuff just makes me more determined. I'm made of pure grit, Corbin, and I'm going to win this whole competition."

She slid off the horse and started walking up the canyon. Corbin dismounted and followed her. He let her walk in silence for a nearly a half mile before pointing off to the east where the shale on the side of a ridge was disturbed. Corbin reached out and grabbed her arm and swung her around so that they were facing each other. He was dangerously close. She jerked her arm, trying to free herself and he stared at her, his eyes no longer laughing.

"You very well may beat me, but don't think for a minute that I'll let you win easy. I'm giving this my all as well, and I too have grit in my blood," Corbin said. "In fact, my blood is so thick with grit it barely flows through my goddamn veins. So let's find this mustang of yours because I'm going to do my best to beat you and I don't want any excuse like 'my horse got lost' to get in the way."

Elsie swiftly kicked him in the shin just above his boot. "Don't you ever touch me again," she said.

"Fair enough," Corbin replied. "Stop being so difficult, though. I'm the one helping you. Plus, I have a horse."

He rubbed his shin and glanced up at her with his full lips pinched together and fire in his eyes. He looked amazingly hot, and she instantly chastised herself for thinking any such thing about her rival and the man who might end up standing between her and her dream of becoming a horse trainer.

"Okay, let's go." She was too mad to tell him thanks and too flustered to admit that he might be right, and she *did* need him.

***

Just as the sun was starting to set, they rode into a valley filled with grass so high it swished against Nighthawk's belly. Standing at the far end, where the hills came together, was Elsie's mustang. He raised his head when he saw them, but stood still with long shoots of the rich grass dangling from his mouth. Corbin untied his lariat from this saddle.

"Wait," Elsie said. "Just let me try something first."

The sun was in her eyes as they approached her horse slowly, in a zigzag fashion. The funny thing about horses, she had learned, was that they saw someone as a predator if they approached in a straight line. She wanted Magic to see her again as one of the herd. A late-afternoon breeze brushed along her forearms, soft as the grass swishing against her boots as she walked. She knew it might take some time to convince the scared mustang that she was a friend. His headlong flight must have been like reliving a nightmare and she didn't know if he was in the proper mindset to remember all the training they had done together.

Thirty feet away, she stopped again, watching and reading the body language of her horse. His eyes were worried. He raised his head, shaking the rope which still dangled from his halter. She eased her weight back onto the leg which was farthest from the horse. She shifted all of her presence back, trying to tell him she did not want to invade his space without his permission. Finally, the horse lowered his head and licked his lips—a sign he was relaxing. Elsie took a few more steps forward but stopped again as soon as Magic acted nervous. This continued for nearly an hour: the horse dictating how close Elsie could get and she respecting his wishes. Overhead, the clouds formed, broke apart, and blew away. The smell of fresh grass, crushed by the horse and girl filled the air. Elsie lost track of time as she slipped into the world that horses inhabited; where sight, sound, taste, and feeling in the moment were the only things that mattered.

When the sun had set and there was only purple light in which the two could see each other, Magic lowered his head and licked his lips. His eyes were soft and relaxed. Elsie reached out and touched his shoulder. He stood, letting her hand caress his silky coat. She stroked his neck and let him sniff her hands. Finally, she grasped the rope. She hoped the bond they had built over the last hour meant something to her wild horse. She turned and headed back toward the silhouette of Corbin and his mount. The mustang followed her, his head down and gait easy and slow.

When they reached Corbin, she expected him to make fun of her slow approach to capturing her mustang. Instead, he simply said, "Good job."

Full dark settled upon them, and only then did Elsie realize they were a few hours' ride, on a fresh horse, away from home. She looked up at Corbin.

"I think we're camping tonight." He spoke in barely more than a whisper, as if he didn't want to break the spell of connection that the valley, now in shadow, had thrown upon the wild horse and humans. "There should be a stream just on the other side of this valley. Should we go see?"

They set off on foot, the horses walking behind them. The moon began to rise as they climbed out of the vale and down the slope on the other side.

The adrenaline from the chase, and then her final play with Magic as she worked to earn his trust, was wearing off. She found her body ached in numerous places. She glanced down at her hands, which were stiff with dried blood. Corbin was silent and she wondered if he was cursing her for the keeping them out after sunset with no food, shelter, or a horse for her to ride home.

Once over the ridge, they dropped down a long, steep hill leading to a small creek. Two old pines grew thirty feet from the bank.

"As good a spot as we'll find." He nodded toward the fast-flowing stream.

"Yes." She was quiet for a moment as they walked the last few hundred feet to the trees. "Thanks for everything. I wouldn't have found my horse without your help."

"Wow, I wish I had my phone to record what you just said." Corbin's tone was light.

"Don't be a jerk and make a big deal out of it." Elsie regretted being honest with him.

"I'm not. I just thought I'd never hear those dear words pass between your lips," Corbin said.

Elsie looked up at him. Something in his tone sounded less adversarial and almost flirtatious—though not in the annoying way to which she had grown accustomed.

"What I mean is, let's have a truce. Okay? For one night let's just act like we're two people camping out under the stars—without a tent, bedrolls, food, or any of that other stuff." He grinned and adjusted his hat. "But anyway, for tonight, let's forget about the whole competition and the past. Let's just be a girl and a guy and make the best of a bad situation. Okay?" He looked earnest.

"Okay," she agreed. Her voice sounded small even to her own ears. She realized without her anger and competitive spirit, she was just worn out and barely holding it all together. She looked away from his face and felt tears sting her eyes. She was silly for being so mean to Corbin when he was helping her so much. Because of her, and her senseless horse, they were both stranded in the dark.

"I'll water the horses and set the hobbles if you'd like?" she offered.

"Sure, I'll see about finding some firewood."

They headed off in opposite directions and by the time Elsie had the horses watered and ready for the night, Corbin had a neat pile of sticks together and was striking sparks off his knife blade with a piece of flint.

"There might be an energy bar in my saddlebag." He spoke as she sat down next to the river rocks he had used to form a fire ring.

Elsie pulled his saddle over and rummaged through the bags fastened to the back of the cantle. She pulled out a lighter, which she handed to Corbin.

He took it with a grin on his face. "This night is starting to look up already."

He had the fire crackling in no time and by the light, she looked deeper in the saddlebag. She pulled out an energy bar, a bandage for a horse, and a condom. She held the condom up.

"What?" Corbin said. His face was the perfect image of boy-like innocence. "I practice safe sex."

"Really? In your saddlebag?" Elsie said.

"Don't forget about our truce." Corbin sounded playful.

Elsie swallowed several retorts. They were bitter going down, but she had agreed to keep the peace. Instead of speaking, she broke the energy bar in half and they ate in silence. Corbin filled his canteen from the creek and after a few gulps, Elsie felt less hungry.

"You can have the saddle blanket," Corbin said.

"No, that's okay. It's my fault we're out here anyway and so you should have it. Without your help, I'd be lost somewhere without my horse or a fire."

"No, really take it," Corbin said. He stood and shook the blanket out on the ground. "Heck, there's even room for both of us. Under the terms of the truce, I won't have wandering hands."

He held both hands up and made a mock-serious face. Elsie could not help but smile, and she felt her shoulders begin to relax. For all his womanizing and high bantering, maybe Corbin really had grown into a pretty decent human being.

"Okay," she said.

She zipped her jacket up all the way to her chin and lay down on her belly, facing the fire. Corbin did the same and their shoulders touched.

"So tell me about this whole thing you were doing with your horse to catch him," Corbin said. "Oh, and by the way, you seriously need to give your mustang another name. Maybe something along the lines of Runs-Like-The-Wind? Or, I know, Hard-To-Catch."

"Stop. I like 'Magic.' I know it's simple and maybe not the most original, but I sort of feel like the two of us have this magic that happens when we're together," Elsie said. "Today wasn't a good example, for sure. But I know he's the hardest horse I've ever had to work with and he's changing me. I think I'm going to be a much better horse trainer because of this boy."

"I know what you mean. Whenever I'm working with a really challenging horse, and we finally make a connection, it does kind of feel like magic." He sat up on his elbows and stirred the fire with a stick. "I'll catch a couple of trout first thing in the morning, so we have something in our stomachs to get us back to the ranch."

"Good, I'm starving. I forget how much I love food until I ride horses and walk all day and then don't have dinner," Elsie said.

"Yeah, I went on a vision quest when I was a kid, about thirteen or fourteen years old. And I seriously didn't eat for three days." Corbin stared into the fire.

"You know, you'd never really tell me anything about growing up on the reservation before."

"I was running pretty hard from my childhood back then."

"You and me both." Elsie pictured the training hospital in Helena. "But what was it like growing up in the mountains, on the reservation?"

"Mostly it was Mom and me just getting by. When my father was around, we traveled from a little rundown house to little rundown trailer. But that was when I was young. Clay's six years older and he was off on the rodeo circuit by the time I was twelve. I got into a little bit of trouble, and so Mom signed me up for a 'spiritual leader.' Basically, I learned about being Lakota, and did sweat lodges and a vision quest."

"Really? Did you see anything?"

"I did."

Elsie watched his face as the light from the fire illuminated a play of emotion she did not understand. For a long moment, she wanted to ask what he might've seen all by himself all those years ago but she stopped herself, suddenly unsure how she could ask.

"I can't imagine. My family is so normal it hurts sometimes," she said instead. Carefully, she looked down at her hands, which were becoming stiff. Dried blood clung to the long rope burns spanning the length of her palms.

"That's all I wanted for most of my childhood." He was still staring into the fire. "To be normal." He shook his head and looked at her. His eyes were dark and very calm. Gently, he took one of her hands in his and examined it in the firelight. "These are pretty deep. They really should be cleaned."

He got up and searched in his saddlebag, then pulled out a small silver flask and shook it before smiling. Elsie sat up and held her hands out.

"This is going to hurt," he warned.

"I know. Just do it." She set her lips.

"Maybe you should have a swig first, to help with the pain?" Corbin said.

"Okay, hand it over."

He handed her the silver flask. As their hands touched, their eyes met. A pulse of electricity shot through her body and she watched his face closely to see if he felt it too. Yes, she saw it register in his eyes, and she quickly looked down. The last thing she needed was to give him the wrong idea. They were still competitors, even if they had drawn a truce for the night. Tomorrow, once they were back at the ranch, it would be business as usual as they both trained their horses to compete against one another.

She pulled the cap off the flask and took a gulp. The liquor burned a trail down her throat and into her chest. She sat still with her eyes closed before handing it back to Corbin.

"Bravo, you still drink like a real cowgirl," he said. He raised the flask to his own lips and took a quick swallow.

"To give me strength for what lies ahead," he said. He winked, then grabbed her hand and poured the liquor across her palm and fingers.

It burned much worse than peroxide. Elsie yelped and tried to snatch her hand back, but Corbin held it firmly in his.

"Another drink?" He offered her the flask with his free hand.

She reached for it and took another gulp, while Corbin captured her other hand. He poured the alcohol across her palm again. This time, she was either ready for the sting or the whiskey, on an empty stomach, was catching up to her. The pain was less and her whole body began to hum with warmth. She sat back on her haunches and rested both of her hands on her knees, palm up. Corbin watched her as he took another sip of the whiskey.

"Better?"

"Yes." Elsie looked up and smiled at him.

He was staring at her and the look in his eyes made her blood run hot, but in a different way than she was used to, the old way.

"You were going to tell me about how you caught the horse-that-might-be-called-Magic," Corbin said.

"Oh, yes." She looked down at her damaged hands. Was she a little disappointed that he had not tried to kiss her? No, she firmly told herself, the last thing she needed was to get tangled up with Corbin Darkhorse again. If they had not agreed to a truce, and if the day had not been so intense, she knew she would not be harboring these strange thoughts toward him.

She needed to clear her mind and so she concentrated on explaining her horse training theory to him. "Have you noticed that horses seem to be able to feel you touch them before you actually do?"

"Yes, all the time. Especially the sensitive ones," Corbin replied.

"Well, when I was working with this one stallion, I started to realize that he had this sort of bubble of 'feel' around his whole body," Elsie said. "And I had to be respectful and pay attention to it if I wanted to get anywhere with him."

"I've never really thought about it like that, but you're right. So when you approached your mustang, you were feeling that bubble around him?"

"Yes, it's like they have layers to the bubble. I can walk right up to Sky, and he won't really feel like I'm in his space until I'm two feet away," she said. "But with Magic, since he doesn't trust me, it's like I have to walk through layers of the bubble. Each time I saw him get uncomfortable, I backed off and gave him time to adjust to my closeness. It was as if I was telling him he had a say in how our relationship progressed, and that made him want to be with me simply because he knew he had a choice in the matter."

Corbin was quiet and they both watched the fire.

"I've not always been very good at giving choices to my horses," he said.

He handed her the flask and she took a sip. The fire crackled and overhead the stars came out and decorated the night sky. Elsie handed the whiskey to Corbin and rolled onto her back in order to see the stars more clearly. A few moments later, Corbin followed her, and they rested together in silence. Elsie felt her eyes grow heavy as the long day and the liquor eased through her tired body. A single coyote let out a wail so piercing and sad Elsie jumped, then impulsively moved closer to Corbin. As if he had been waiting all night for this moment, he snugged her up to his body and rested his head on his crooked arm. Their faces were only inches apart. Elsie could feel her heart beating as loud and fast as a herd of galloping horses. Perhaps the whiskey was making her bold and careless but she reached out and touched his high, smooth cheek. He matched her movement, his own fingers light as moth wings on her skin. His touch left trails of warmth and made her stomach tighten deliciously.

"Oh, cowboy, you think I'm like all the girls at the rodeo—lined up waiting for a tumble in the hay with the

Lakota Horse Trainer?" Elsie said. Her tone was light and she took a deep breath to try to slow her thundering heart.

"No, I actually don't think you're like any of those girls. But—" He hesitated, lifting one eyebrow, letting his very nearness to her do its work. "But, I think you're a hot-blooded woman, a strong-willed woman, and I think you know what you want. That's sexy as hell. But I also think you aren't being completely honest with yourself when it comes to me."

"You really are incredibly arrogant," Elsie said.

"So you've told me." He grinned. "If I have no effect on you anymore, why not let me try and seduce you? Why not see if I still have what it takes?"

"What? No, that's just stupid."

"Are you scared you can't resist me?" Corbin asked.

She could see his smile and his eyes were alive with more than just firelight. As she crossed her arms over her chest, she knew she wanted to let him try. It had been so long since anyone had touched her. She could remember what it was like to let his fine-boned hands ran down her sides; to surrender to his touch and fire and very nearness. For the time being, her brain was blocking out all the hurt and pain that had constituted the end of their summer together. As the night closed in and the sky lit with more and more stars, she remembered only that he had been the first person to match her passion for life, horses, and then together they had discovered each other. Something deep in her body had awakened and Corbin had become her mate and equal in all things.

"Okay, you're on. But this is a onetime deal. Tomorrow we go back to being competitors. I'm not giving you an inch of ground and the truce will be over," Elsie said. "Plus, I don't think you have what it takes, anyway."

"Deal," Corbin said. She saw the flash of his white teeth in the dark.

He had hurt her and now she wanted only to hurt him back.

CHAPTER FIVE

Corbin gathered Elsie even closer. She could feel his breath, warm and mixed with the smell of whiskey and honey. Gently, so, so, gently, Corbin let his lips graze hers. The feather-kiss sent whispers of excitement down her spine. Again, he brushed his lips over hers before dipping his head and deepening the kiss. He opened his mouth and slid the tip of his tongue over her lips until she opened and let him in.

His tongue was pure fire and swifter now. He moved to brace himself above her. She let her hands wander across his broad shoulders and over his back. He was lean and long-muscled and her hands loved the feel of him. He had been just growing into manhood the last time she had felt his body. Now, with the passage of years, he had filled out the lankiness of youth. Her body loved the feel of him. She moaned low in the back of her throat as he tangled his hand in her hair. He cupped the back of her neck, lifting her up to meet his kiss.

When he pulled back, she could see the stars above them shining even more brilliantly than before. She willed her breathing to not give away her growing excitement.

"I've wanted to do that since the day you told me off at

the mustang pickup," Corbin whispered. He sat up and then reached down to pull Elsie to a sitting position. He lifted her until she was resting on his lap and they faced each other.

"Really?" Elsie said. "I wanted to punch you in the stomach."

"I bet you did." He trapped both of her wrists behind her back in one of his hands and grinned.

With his other hand, he undid the top button of her shirt, still smiling. With her pulse racing, Elsie tried to keep her expression emotionless.

"Your eyes were almost on fire that day. I even thought for a moment that your hair would suddenly combust," Corbin said. He tightened his grip on her wrists and pulled her into his chest so that their faces were mere inches apart. He rubbed his cheek along her bare neck, sending shivers of pleasures shooting down her arms and the backs of her legs.

"I think I've found the best way to hold you," he said next to her ear. "Very, very, carefully."

Then he took her earlobe in his teeth and nipped, before leaving a trail of tiny love bites down her neck. Elsie gasped; this man was turning her resolve into melted spring snow. He pulled away, searching her face.

"How am I doing?"

"If you have to ask, it probably isn't a good sign," Elsie said. She tried desperately to remember all the reasons she detested Corbin Darkhorse. The last thing his enormous ego needed was to realize how much he still affected her.

"God, you're sexy and smart-alecky," He laughed and brushed his lips over her collarbone. She didn't mean to, but her head rolled back to grant him better access to her delicate décolleté.

"I think you're bluffing, that's what I think," Corbin said. "I think my lips are making it hard for you to breathe and your heart is beating so fast it sounds like Magic is running loose again."

"Oh, really? I underestimated the size of your ego," she replied.

"Okay, fair enough. How about you prove you're immune to me? How about you undress *me*." He stared at her, his eyes catching the light from the fire.

In answer, Elsie pulled her wrists free of his hold and sat back on her haunches. Free of his touch, she could think again. She smiled and pushed him down, then in one swift movement tore open his shirt.

"Good," he said. "Now, run your hand very slowly across my chest and down to the little patch of hair, here." With his free hand, he indicated a patch of black hair below his navel, just visible before the waistband of his jeans.

"No, this was not part of the deal," Elsie said. "You can't tell me what to do."

"Come on, we're just having fun. This should be easy since you don't think I'm attractive," Corbin said.

"Fine." She decided not to make a big deal out of it.

She did want to touch the expanse of lean muscle she had uncovered. He lay stretched out before her, shoulders broad and abs rippled waves of perfection. The firelight played across his dark skin, making him look like a Lakota demigod. Her fingers were hesitant as she touched the hollow below his windpipe. The bolt of pure electricity that shot through her body made her withdraw her hand as quickly as if she had touched one of the coals from the fire burning beside them.

"What?" His voice was so low and intimate. He caught her hand in both of his and pressed it back against his bare skin.

She pulled free and steeled herself; running her fingers slowly over his chest. She let them drift down into the place between his pectoral muscles and then travel over his taut stomach, to finally rest on the tiny patch of dark hair. Desperately, she tried to slow her ragged breathing but when she looked up and met his eyes in the firelight, she knew he heard her shallow gulps for air. He sat up and pulled her against him with one arm while the other hand brushed her long hair back from her face. He tilted her chin up so that he could see her eyes.

"You'll be mine?" he said. He must have felt her begin to stiffen because he quickly added, "Just for tonight."

She nodded.

"Can you whisper 'yes' in my ear?"

"Yes." She barely breathed the word against his neck, her nostrils flaring as she took in his scent mixed with wood smoke and saddle soap.

He was released by her single word of consent. Once again, he pulled her onto his lap. This time he used both his hands to lift her up so that he could bury his face in her neck, and lick, kiss, and nip along her hair line and then forward until he was nose-deep in the place between her breasts. Elsie locked her knees around his hips and pushed against his bare chest.

"Lay down," she said.

"Yes, ma'am." He wrapped his arms around Elsie and fell back, taking her with him. When they landed, she was still straddling him around the waist, her hands positioned on either side of his face.

Corbin undid the last three buttons on her shirt and tossed it into the dark. His fingers moved across her bare skin. She didn't even try to control the low growl that emanated from her throat as this sleek, sexy man stroked her bare skin.

"I love that sound," he said. "Make it again."

In answer, she leaned down and kissed him, hard, then grabbed the top button on his worn jeans and started to undo it.

"Whoa, now," Corbin said. He bucked under her, throwing her off balance and then twisted like a wild bronc, catching her with his hands then effortlessly reversing their positions.

"Hi," he said. His lips were a mere inch from her own

as he rested on his elbows above her. "New bet: the first one to, well, to 'reach satisfaction' has to teach the other a training trick they use on their mustang."

Her breathing sounded ragged even to her own ears, and Elsie smiled. "You're on. I don't know how smart it is for you to bet against a lady about that. But I'll take your wager."

"Oh, dear girl. Don't you remember? I can go all night." And with that, he lowered his head to her stomach and left a trail of damp kisses to the waistband of her jeans. He pulled them undone quickly, turning them inside out as he freed her legs in one economical gesture. Nearly naked beneath him, the cool night air no longer felt chill on her aroused skin. She grasped his shaggy head in both her hands as he lipped at her cotton panties. She would have to slow this man down and use all her skills if she would win this thing tonight. Pulling her long hair out from under her shoulders, she let it fan out around her head on the saddle blanket. Then she wrapped her legs around his neck and locked her knees so that she could roll over and position herself above Corbin in a quick and effective judo move. He fought her and then gave in, his white teeth flashing in the light as Elsie settled on his chest, her legs still wrapped around his neck.

"Okay, you win for now. Have your way with me," he said.

Elsie's hair curtained them both as she pinned Corbin's arms above his head. Filtered firelight turned Corbin's skin to gold under her hands. For one long moment, she let her fingertips luxuriate in the feel of him. She knew she couldn't afford to let herself drift too far into the passion she felt just below the surface of her steely control.

She slithered further back on his torso until her knees gripped his ribs. Only then did she dip her head and kiss along the hollow she had discerned just below his windpipe. She trailed her lips over his jaw until she reached his ear.

"I'm going to make all your dreams come true, cowboy. And then you're going to tell me your training secrets," she said. Her lips hovered next to his ear.

He groaned, pulled his hands free of her entrapment, and grabbed her shapely bottom, his hands cupping her perfectly.

"I'm not giving up that easily. Even though you look sexy as hell sitting above me with your wild hair and the fire in your eyes," he said. "You have such a great ass." He added the last as an afterthought, a grin spreading across his face.

He pinched her just a little and when she pulled away from his hands, he drew her body down so they were once again face-to-face. This time when he kissed her, the night around them disappeared and she was lost.

His hands touched her everywhere, fiery and warm. She wanted to resist; somewhere deep inside she could feel the memories from the past. All the pain and loneliness was just waiting and stewing.

She vaguely knew he was pulling her free of her plain, cotton underwear and then her bra. Her body moved with his to ease the removal of her last garments. Her own fingers were desperate to unbutton his jeans and when she finally pulled them undone and slid her hand into the warmth, she was rewarded with the long hardness of him. He grabbed her hand before she could pull his erection free of his pants and he held her wrists in a strong, unbreakable grip. He kissed her bare nipples, taking one in his teeth until she cried and arched her back into his body.

He turned away from her and searched in the saddlebag for the foil-wrapped condom.

"Now, I bet you're glad I ride prepared," he said.

"You have a better chance of winning this thing if you don't talk," Elsie said.

"So now you're giving me pointers? Maybe you do want me to win after all."

She could see something soft and tender in his eyes.

"I've thought about how this might play out for years," he admitted. "Elsie, I'm sorry about before. I was a stupid kid."

He looked down at his hands. Her throat tightened. The heat of passion and his nearly-naked body had kept her warm but suddenly she shivered in the night air. Corbin had proven himself untrustworthy in the past. Why trust him again? The whole situation seemed stupid and futile.

Anger tightened in her chest where only moments before she had felt desire. With his apology, she was again seventeen, her world crumbling around her.

As he unwrapped the condom, Elsie reached for her shirt and jacket, and her skin was icy. What in the hell was she doing, forgetting who he was and also the woman she had become?

Without his hands on her, their skin touching, she was clear-headed.

"I'm done, you win. Ask me whatever secret you want to know and I'll tell you." She hunted around next to the saddle blanket and found her underwear, which she slipped on quickly.

"What's wrong?" Corbin said. "Don't get mad."

Elsie could have sworn he actually looked sorry, and gentle. She never thought she would use that word to describe Corbin Darkhorse. He ran his hand through his hair and looked off at the stream and dark shadows of hills framed by the sky.

"Elsie." She thought she could hear longing in his voice.

"It was fun, but we both know this isn't going anywhere past tonight," she said hurriedly.

"If I could go back, I would." He was staring at her and she looked down.

"Why even start?" Elsie said. She tried as best she could to wrap the shreds of her anger around her. The softness of his eyes was making her resolve waver.

There was a long pause. The connection of electricity she had felt flowing between them just moments earlier was long gone. The night air was chill on her skin.

"Yeah. I'm sure you're right." He grabbed his shirt and buttoned it back into place. "I'm going to go check on the horses."

He disappeared into the dark and Elsie sat on the saddle blanket alone. For having just made the smart choice, she felt incredibly empty and sad.

***

She woke cold. The sky was predawn gray and the fire had burned down to hot coals. Shivering, she got up and searched for more firewood to add to the fire. She had not realized he was behind her until she bumped into him with branches in her hands. He put his arms around her and held her, sticks and all.

"You're cold, aren't you?" His voice was husky with sleep.

"Yes," she said.

"Okay, I'll get more wood and then we'll cuddle." He paused before adding, "For warmth, of course."

They stacked the fire high with fresh wood and then Elsie lay back down on the saddle blanket. Corbin lay behind her and carefully enfolded her in his arms. Involuntarily, she sighed. The warmth from his body felt wonderful and her stiff limbs relaxed.

"Better?" He spoke next to her ear.

"Yes," she whispered. Last night seemed so distant.

Right at the edge of sleep, she heard him say, "You did the right thing, stopping us earlier. Two headstrong people like us in bed again might just burn down the whole forest."

CHAPTER SIX

Corbin woke as the sun crested the hills. The valley by the creek was filled with the soft mist of morning. The horses were pale ghosts to the left of the smoldering fire. He shifted a little and looked down to where Elsie nestled against his side. Her eyelashes were soft shadows on her tanned cheeks. He wanted to brush his fingers along her skin but knew his touch would wake her and end this unusual moment. She was gentle and innocent in sleep; once again the seventeen-year-old girl he had met that fated summer. For a moment, he let himself imagine they were a couple again and that he now held her because they had made love the previous night. He again saw her skin glowing in the warm light of the fire, and her hair loose on her shoulders. He felt the grip of her hands on his arms as she pinned him and saw her grin of triumph as she sat astride his torso. The dark swell of passion in her eyes had stopped him, made him suck in his breath and linger. She was no longer a young girl. There was strength as she had grown into a fierce woman and he desired her more than he had before.

The fantasy was tantalizing, and he could almost convince himself it was real. He had built a career on perpetuating fantasy—the grand prix dressage horse for the elderly lady, the Arabian stallion for the backyard owner. These people came to him and he gave them the illusion of hope when they were really over-mounted and needed a level-headed and less athletic animal to be their partner. He had not realized that his own dream-weaving was making its way into his personal life. But of course it made sense. As he had run, run fast and hard, he had woven a tale, convincing himself she was better off without him in her life. What injured girl needed a dark-skinned cowboy with nothing to his name but a couple saddle horses and a worn-out truck? It was better for her that he leave, better for everyone. The look her parents had given him said it all: he was to blame. This, he knew was true. She had met him when she was full of fire and youth and a great deal too much trust, and he had stumbled and walked away when she needed him most.

The birds were waking. A red-winged blackbird let out a chorus of beautifully trilled notes. Corbin wished the moment could go on and on. He shifted a bit more so that he could rest her closer to his chest. The problem with youth, he realized, was that it was hard to understand how important each moment really was. He was not naïve enough to think he and Elsie would have easily sailed through the past decade. Perhaps they would have fought and broken up anyway. What bothered him was how he had left her when she was vulnerable and needed him and how, no matter how much he apologized to her, his past actions spoken much louder than his current words.

He didn't have any other regrets. In fact, he prided himself on being a man who was fully present in the moment. The problem was that Elsie despised him in the present. At least, he reasoned, she was at the ranch for the next three months. He had no doubt she would do her best to beat him in the competition and even though he acted very confident, he imagined she probably would win. He would never presume to think he should let her win;

she was an amazing horse trainer and someone who definitely did not need any extra help from him.

She opened her eyes. For one sleep-softened moment, she met his gaze with openness. He thought he detected joy in her eyes.

Then she blinked and rolled away from him. "Sorry, I guess I got cold." Her voice was low.

"It's okay. I'm sorry about last night." His arms felt empty.

"My fault too. I guess that's what happened when there's history, even if it's old and bad."

"Hopefully you don't remember all of it as bad?" He knew he was pushing his luck.

She stood and looked down at him for a long questioning moment. "I know you're sorry."

"Then forgive me." He spoke with more force than he had intended.

"I do." She looked away to the horses when she spoke. He felt as if she was far away. A surge of anger made him clench his fists. He knew he had only himself to blame, but still, Elsie was the hardest-headed woman he'd ever met. He pulled his boots on and ran a hand through his hair. Elsie was heading to the creek and he busied himself with checking the horses over and putting dirt on the smoldering fire. She returned, her hair damp and skin bright from the cold water. They saddled Nighthawk in complete silence. Briefly, he wondered if he was truly this bad at communicating, or maybe this stubborn woman made him this tongue-tied and frustrated. He had built a whole career around communicating with both horses and humans, but now he seemed lost as to how to open up to her in the way she seemed to need. He wanted to be angry and blame her. As their hands touched when she handed him the cinch, he thought about doing just that. How much easier to stomp off; he had offered his apology. It was no longer his problem if she couldn't forgive him. He kept his face expressionless as he bridled the Nighthawk.

The mustang seemed soft and docile in the cool morning light. Elsie had done a great job with the horse, and he felt himself smile just a little and when he looked up he found her watching him. She matched his smile.

"Thank you." She seemed sincere and he felt his heart soften even further. He knew he would keep trying to win her back, show her that he was trustworthy and strong. A man she could count on. He took a deep breath. Sometimes those hell hounds still liked to whimper and whine around his feet, skulking only the way the past ever could.

***

As Corbin and Elsie rode double-down the last descent to Bear Dance Ranch, with Magic ponied up behind them, they were met by Byron, Clay, and Annie on horseback.

"Thank goodness you're all right," Annie called out as they the two groups got closer.

"Was it that ridiculous plane that scared him?" Byron said.

"Yes," Elsie replied.

"We lost the light after we caught the mustang," Corbin interjected. "So we had to stay put for the night."

Nighthawk whinnied to the other horses, and they all stopped and stood together, the morning sun bright-gold and clear.

"Sorry, he got loose," Elsie said. She nodded back to a now docile Magic.

"We're just glad you're okay," Annie said again.

"Her hands are pretty burnt up." Corbin sounded concerned and she saw him hover his hand above her thigh as if he were about to touch her.

"Oh no. Can I see?" Anna urged her horse closer.

Elsie held her hands out, palms up. They looked a little better after their whiskey treatment the previous night.

"We'll get you bandaged up with some salve," Annie

said. "Do they hurt much?"

"Not really," Elsie replied. "Corbin poured some whiskey over them last night and that actually helped."

Clay was giving Corbin the stare only a brother can give. Elsie felt tired and in need of breakfast and a bath.

"Well, let's get back to the ranch and have some food," Byron said. "The guests will want to hear all about your wild mustang chase since they missed their moonlight ride on account of it."

"Gosh, I'm so sorry," Elsie said. She looked down at her worn-out boots.

"Actually, I think they would like hearing you and Corbin tell your story more than any trail ride anyway," Clay said. "Now, come on. Lenora is making pancakes with banana and walnut drizzle. And elk sausage."

"We better hurry," Corbin said. "Lenora never makes sausage."

Byron was still grumbling about the plane. He turned his horse and as they all headed back to the ranch, he said, "I'm placing a complaint with the FAA. Whoever owns that plane could have gotten someone seriously hurt. Or even worse." Urging his horse forward, he gave Elsie a quick smile. "You're part of the Bear Dance family now. We take care of our own."

Even though she was tired, hungry, and cold, Elsie felt warmth in her heart. These people whom she hardly knew had taken her in so generously and now treated her as one of their own.

Over breakfast, Elsie and Corbin told the story of their adventure to the two families staying at the ranch. Elsie held up her torn hands as evidence.

One small boy with a vivid imagination asked, "How did you stay warm?"

"Yes," Clay said. "I was actually wondering that myself."

Lenora elbowed Clay in the side. "Don't push it right

now," she said almost under her breath.

"We had a fire," Corbin replied. He looked right at Clay and Elsie looked at her half-eaten pancake.

"That's it?" Clay said. He had a smile on his lips and his eyes were bright. "I remember me and Lenora getting caught in a freak storm and sheltering in a cave. That was quite a night."

Lenora smiled, her face glowing as she turned toward Clay. Elsie looked down as Lenora ran her fingertips lightly over Clay's high cheekbones. Last night was still too raw, her nerves were singing with the close proximity to the other Darkhorse brother. She had to put some distance between the two of them.

"We cuddled to share our body heat," Elsie said. There was no reason not to face the truth head-on. "That's what you have to do if you are caught out at night in the mountains. You have to cuddle up with the person you are with and share the warmth from your body." She smiled at the guests. The kids nodded. Her neck and cheeks felt hot. She knew Corbin was staring at her. She cut her pancake into bite-sized pieces and took a deep breath. Somehow, yesterday, Magic's flight and Corbin's instantaneous help had made her question her own motives. She hated not being able to trust her own judgment, but when it came to Corbin, nothing added up the way it should. The pancakes smelled of maple syrup and she chewed slowly. She just needed to keep her eye on the goal, then she could have her own place and she would never have to see Corbin Darkhorse again.

After breakfast dishes, Elsie made her way to her own trailer to shower and find fresh clothes. Outside in the morning sunlight, she ran her fingers through her damp hair. The wind had picked up a little and high clouds scuttled through the blue sky. As she walked back toward the main barns to get started on chores, Elsie saw Lenora wave to her from the front porch. She walked back to the large ranch house.

"Would you like to help Annie and me with some pies?" Lenora added quickly when she saw Elsie's hesitation, "It will be fun, just us ladies and plenty of test-tasting to do."

"Okay," Elsie said. "I've never made a pie before."

"It's really easy and always more fun when there are a few of us and we can chat."

Annie set a bowl of dough on the counter in front of Elsie. "Grab some flour out of that jar and dust your workspace and hands," she said. "Then grab the rolling pin." Annie smiled. "Keep even pressure." She placed her hands over Elsie's and gently pressed down.

Elsie knew her face must have looked worried. Annie patted her shoulder "You'll do just fine."

Lenora was humming under her breath as she mixed blackberries and peaches together with maple syrup and cinnamon.

"How do you feel?" Elsie blurted out.

Lenora turned and smiled. "Big," she said.

Elsie tried not to put too much pressure on the rolling pin as she felt her cheeks turning red. She felt useless in the kitchen, surrounded by these confident and capable women. She wanted only the mountain air and a difficult horse.

"That pie dough looks about thin enough," Lenora said. "Set a pan on the sheet and then lift up."

Elsie did as she was directed and smiled as the thin sheet of dough filled the glass pie pan perfectly. Then she went to smooth the edge down and a jagged line appeared through the middle. Elsie froze.

"It's fine," Lenora said. "Pinch the seam like this." She used her fingers to gently draw the torn edges together. "It will still taste just as good. And no one will even know."

"I'm so bad at all this stuff," Elsie said. "My mom used to always send me out to the barn with Dad."

"You'll get better," Lenora said reassuringly.

"We need you more now than ever," Annie said. She set down another bag of frozen berries on the counter. "Lenora will be down with the baby and we need to have as many capable hands on this ranch as possible."

"I'll keep trying, but I feel so useless in the kitchen," Elsie said. She knew her voice had a whiny edge and wished she could change it.

It had seemed to Elsie that all during her childhood, she had never fit in with her sisters and mother. She had the same feeling now as Annie and Lenora easily moved around each other. They were laughing, their bodies relaxed. Elsie took a deep breath; her own shoulders were tight with stress. She felt as if she did not belong. For a long moment, tears pricked her eyelids. It was foolish to cry, she knew, and yet she felt as if her whole life she had somehow been fighting her way toward a future which now felt lonely and empty. Yet she had no idea how to stop fighting. It felt as if the whole world was always trying to stop her and so for that very reason Elsie fought on. As she kneaded dough in the kitchen and the sun shots rays of heavy, golden light through the windows over the sink, she wondered, for the first time, if she were to stop fighting, what would really happen. Would she slide back down the mountain?

"Add the berry mixture," Lenora instructed.

Elsie let her hands steady with the task and her mind ease into the flow of the ranch kitchen. She had fought so hard for so long that she had no idea who was even against her anymore.

***

Clay pulled Corbin outside to help with a sickly calf.

"I hope you were a gentleman last night?" Clay said.

"Yes, pretty much," Corbin replied. He tried not to remember the firelight dancing on Elsie's bare skin.

"Good, that's one heck of a girl, little brother. If you

had any sense at all, you'd wake up and see that."

"Oh, I see it," Corbin said. "I don't think she really likes me a whole lot right now."

"Well, quit acting like a grade-A jerk all the time and she might change her mind," Clay said. "What happened back on the circuit?"

"I was young." Corbin pulled a protesting calf away from its mother. "I wasn't there when she probably needed me most."

"The limp?" Clay asked.

"Yes." Corbin didn't want to look up and meet his brother's eyes. Instead, he readied the needle. "She broke her femur in two places and shattered her pelvis."

Clay let out a low whistle. "Brave girl. That mustang she has now doesn't look too gentle."

"I know." Corbin's face registered his fear and frustration. "I can't tell her how worried I am. Every time I try, she takes it as a challenge and barges forward while cussing me under her breath."

Clay snorted. "She's almost spitting fire most of the time when she looks at you."

"I know." Corbin found himself smiling. "She's always had a way with horses. Nothing pretend about her and the animals just sort of sense it. I guess I just have to trust that she'll be okay this time."

"You're going to have to use more than your looks to get her back," Clay said. He held the calf steady as Corbin administered the shot.

They both straightened up, releasing the youngster. He ran back to his mother and began to nurse.

"You do know how to do that, right? Use more than that pretty face of yours to win a woman?" Clay's tone was very big-brother-knows-best.

"I'll figure her out."

"Don't wait too long. Someone else might find her before you get your act together."

"I already told you, I'm trying." Corbin was irritated.

He hoped he would not blow it this time around with the woman who was as wild as the horses they were supposed to be breaking.

CHAPTER SEVEN

Magic's runaway had facilitated a new bond between Elsie and her mustang. He watched her now with a softness in his large expressive eyes that seemed to assure her he knew she was on his side. More and more frequently, he moved toward her like a domestic horse and watched her with an equine affection expressed by gentle blows through his elegantly flared nostrils or an occasional shake of his black mane.

Elsie ran her hands over his body before directing him out onto a circle. The sun was lowering to the west and the light had taken on the golden, saturated color she so loved. She absently watched as a car drove down the long gravel road leading to the ranch. She let Magic circle closer to her and then stop so that he too could watch the approaching vehicle. With her horse trailer and round pen tucked away behind the barns and protected by the small hill and pond, she didn't realize the car belonged to her mother until it stopped and the driver's side door opened. Elsie took a deep breath. She had not charged her cell phone in a few days and realized too late that her mother would have worried about her lack of communication.

"Hi, Mom." She tried to make her voice sound

cheerful.

"Elsie, answer your phone." Lina Rosewood looked less than happy. "You are breaking a wild horse again and yet not responding to my messages?"

"I'm sorry, Mom." Elsie touched Magic's nose. "I forgot to charge my phone." She didn't add that she had spent the previous night out in the mountains after the aforementioned wild horse ran away.

Lina rested her elbows on the round pen rails. She carefully removed her sunglasses and Elsie instantly felt bad as she realized her mother looked worried and a little tired.

"I'm sorry, Mom. I know it's a long drive." She opened the corral gate and let her mother inside. Carefully, she wrapped her arms around the other woman.

"Elsie, you're riding wild horses again. Don't you realize how much this worries me?"

"Can you just be happy for me?" Elsie said. "For once?"

"I am," Lina said. She stepped away and looked at Elsie. Her beautifully shaped brows pulled together made her look closer to her fifty-nine years.

"Don't you see?" her mother continued. "I want you to be happy, of course, but I also want you to be safe."

"I know you do," Elsie replied. "It's just that I sometimes wish I could be like Hazel and Kate. But I can't. I really am put together this way."

The mustang nuzzled his way between them. Elsie watched as her mother's face softened and a smile played around her lips. Magic touched her mother's hands with his velvet black muzzle. He was curious to meet this new person holding Elsie's attention.

"He is a sweet horse. I can tell you've worked hard to earn his trust."

"I have, Mom. I'm going really slow with him and letting him take an active role in his own education. He's learning how to live in this new human-world and he's really trying hard."

"Good." Lina withdrew her hand from the mustang and touched Elsie's cheek. "You'll be careful this time?"

"Yes, of course. Believe me, I don't want to end up in the hospital again."

"I know you don't, Elsie." Her mother hesitated, lowered her hand, and then looked off toward the lowering sun. "I thought I had put it to rest, you know, the fear that turned my whole body to ice that day they brought you into the ER. But when I saw you took on another mustang, I felt it all over again. I woke up this morning sick to my stomach and knew I had to track you down."

With her mother's words, Elsie could smell hospital sheets, disinfected, bleached, and then starched. Her stomach tightened with the fear of a past trauma that she was reminded of every day, with every step she took. The memory, of the time after the wild horse had trampled her, came rushing back with the force of an untamed mustang fighting for freedom.

When she woke up, her body was numb. For a long moment, she thought the accident had been a dream and then she tried to move her legs and a slow, hot pain worked its way up and twisted through her stomach. She groaned. Very slowly, she rolled her head to the side and tried to look around the hospital room. White walls with a blue chair rail, one empty chair next to the bed. The door opened and her mother came in, dressed in scrubs and her eyes red-rimmed and face drawn. Elsie realized it was bad. Her mother sat on the edge of the bed. Elsie smelled the rosewater soap her mother washed her face with every morning, and the smell grounded her in the moment even as a hard lump filled her throat.

"My angel." Her mother's voice was hoarse. "Does it hurt?"

"A little." Elsie pushed the rising lump in her throat back down and swallowed. Her tongue felt thick and dry. "Can I have some water?"

"Yes." Her mother brought a plastic cup and straw up to Elsie's

lips.

She realized tears were running down her mother's cheeks.

A dread so deep and hard filled her chest that she had to speak. "Are my legs okay?"

Her mother reached down and held Elsie's hand. The tears were dripping onto the white hospital spread, staining the cloth with wet blotches.

Her mother cried harder. She ran her hands along Elsie's face. The lump filled her chest and she tried to get air.

Her mother straightened up, her hands still cupping Elsie's face. "Your right leg was badly crushed. You have a pin in your hip and rod running the length of your femur."

Elsie closed her eyes and for a long moment, she willed herself to not cry. Her mind ran wild circles. She tried to wiggle her feet. She jerked the bedspread to the side as best she could. Her arms felt as heavy as chunks of firewood but she managed to pull the blanket free. A wave of nausea washed over her and she turned her head and nearly retched over the side of the hospital bed. Her mother held her hair and brushed her hands along her back. When the gagging subsided, she lay on the pillow, exhausted, tears trapped in the corners of her eyes and yet refusing to fall.

"Where's Corbin?" she asked once she trusted her voice.

"He was here the first night. I don't know now." Her mother stood. Her face was still tired but now arranged. Elsie knew she was turning on her nurse-mode.

"The horse?" she asked.

"They had to euthanize her."

"Will I ride again?" She barely dared to ask.

"I don't think so. But," her mother hurried to add. "you might walk again, with time."

Elsie nodded. She closed her eyes and the darkness of oblivion was waiting for her.

"I'm sorry." Elsie felt her throat tighten. The memory was so fresh and raw even a decade later. "I'm scared too, but I want this and I want to try again. I don't mean to hurt you or make you worry. I'm just trying, in my own awkward way, to forge a life for myself."

Lina wrapped her arms around Elsie and for a long moment, they were silent. Elsie doubted her mother would ever understand the strange urge that she felt to ride these wild horses. Sometimes, she did not fully understand her own desires.

"This time is different," she promised. "This time is about healing." She knew as the words left her mouth that they were true.

"Yes," Lina said. "I think you might be right."

They stood together for a long time in silence, two humans and a black mustang.

Finally, Lina spoke. "I better get back."

"You could stay for dinner?" Elsie said.

"Another night," her mother replied.

Elsie walked with her to the car, Magic trailing along behind them.

"You really have worked a miracle with this horse."

"Thanks," Elsie said.

"I'm proud of you. I really am." Then her mother closed the car door and put on her sunglasses before pulling out of the ranch. Elsie stood and watched.

***

At sunset, Elsie and Corbin waited outside the large outdoor arena on their horses, Sky and Nighthawk. The guests and a few neighbors sipped lemonade or wine in Adirondack chairs. Elsie wiped her damp palm on her pant leg. It had been so long since she had performed in front of a crowd. Even if this one was small, she still found her stomach clenching. Without meaning to, she glanced at Corbin. He nodded when he saw her watching him. Even though his eyes were shaded by his hat, she thought he looked a little nervous as well.

Annie started the music and they cantered their horses into the arena, and then performed a sliding stop in unison. There was some mild clapping from the sidelines. Together, they urged their horses into a canter in the opposite direction. Riding side by side, they pulled their horses close. Elsie could feel the thrusts of power with each stride Sky took. She quieted her rapidly beating heart and concentrated on Corbin's steady hands. Elsie threw a leg over Corbin's horse and then pushed free of her own galloping animal. She grabbed the back of his saddle and hung on as Corbin used the horn on Elsie's saddle and swung onto Sky. The crowd whistled and clapped and Elsie felt herself begin to smile. They switched back to their own horses while still cantering. Elsie looked up to meet Corbin's gaze for a split second and thought she saw admiration in his eyes. She looked down, disconcerted. Somehow, his opinion had started to matter to her again. Or worse, it always had. She forced herself to concentrate only on the music; this was no time to let the past become the present.

The music changed and became slower. She slowed Sky to a halt and then dismounted and pulled off the saddle and bridle. Once her tack was removed, she asked her horse to lie down. All the while, Corbin began to put a larger and larger loop on his lariat as he loped his horse in a big circle around Elsie and Sky. Once her horse was lying down, Elsie climbed onto his back and then bumped his side gently with her calves for him to stand. She stretched out her leg, letting her damaged pelvis shift as best it could to sitting on a horse bareback. Taking a deep breath, she moved him into a canter. The wind was kicking up from the west. Elsie's hair blew sideways, mixing with Sky's mane.

Corbin widened his loop even further. Using only her knees and calves, Elsie guided Sky toward the expanding lariat. She ran her fingers through her horse's blowing mane then urged him forward and up. In one smooth motion, horse and rider jumped through the spinning loop.

Everyone stood and clapped. Elsie and Corbin had kept their routine private and so it was a surprise for the entire Bear Dance family and not just the guests. Elsie was smiling so big her cheeks hurt. She turned to Corbin to see her grin mirrored on his face. He winked and lifted his hand, fingers spanning wide and palm toward her. She met his eyes and then touched her hand to his. They did make one hell of a good team, she thought. Just then the boom of thunder and a flash of lightning lit the night sky to the west.

"Quick to the dining hall for dessert!" Lenora called.

Everyone started packing up and Corbin and Elsie rode their horses back to the barns alone. Halfway up the big hill, the heavens opened and a drenching rain began to fall. The horses put their heads down and Elsie and Corbin urged them into the shelter of the barn. Once inside, the sound of rain falling on the tin roof effectively closed them off from the rest of the world. They dismounted and untacked their horses, pulling wet tack and saddle blankets from the animals. Steam rose from equine skin, sweat-dampened and then rain-soaked. Elsie smelled pine shavings and the richness of dust wetted and turned to Montana mud. Her heart was light and even though her hip tingled and burned just a little—the way it often did after riding a horse bareback. The pure contentment, which came from being fully connected to her equine partner, flowed through her body, dulling any discomfort. Outside the barn door, a curtain of rain shielded horses and humans from the rest of the world.

Elsie moved around her Sky, running her hands over his damp coat. She looked up and saw Corbin standing perfectly still, rainwater dripping from his hair and dark eyelashes.

She realized he was reading her the same way he did a wild mustang. He reached out and touched her cheek, brushed his fingers down her jaw, and then ran his thumb across her lips. She grabbed his hand and stilled his movement. He reached for her, his fingers firm against her ribs as he pulled her into him. With one hand, he pressed the small of her back until she was snug against his wet body. She tensed, ready to push away from him, ready to fight and shove and kick.

With his free hand, he tucked a strand of her dripping hair behind her ear.

"I love the way you look damp from the rain," he whispered. His eyes were shot through with tiny green flecks as she stared back at him.

"I don't think I've ever seen you lost for words before, El."

A raindrop dripped down the back of her neck, weaving a cold trail down her spine. She blinked. The spell was broken. Alone in the barn with Corbin Darkhorse and somehow she had allowed herself, once again, to be caught up in his enchantment.

"I'm not," Elsie said. "We better put the horses away."

"Yes, of course." He dropped his arms as she pulled back and then stepped away from him.

They avoided eye contact the whole way to the corral. This was the closest they had been since their single-night truce after catching the runaway Magic. Elsie put her head down, letting her hair curtain her face. In that moment, she did not trust the swirl of emotions moving through her body. The best way to interact with the man, who had abandoned her all those years ago, was at arm's length.

CHAPTER EIGHT

The next morning, Elsie took a group of guests out for a ride along the river. The sky was a brilliant blue and cloudless, the rain had given the world a clean feel, and swallows swooped in front of the horses. She took a deep breath and felt her heart lift and soar. She knew she was ridiculously lucky to be riding a horse on such a fine day. As she glanced back at the two mothers, with their daughters mounted by their sides, she saw her own joy, at the beautiful morning, reflected in each face. The world was alive and fresh that fine day. Staying at Bear Dance Ranch had been the best choice she had made in a long time. Maybe, she thought, things were changing for the better. The last ten years had been such a struggle and, at least for the morning, it was good to relax and just let the flow of life move her along.

As the small group of five riders and horses made their way back to the ranch, Elsie noticed a truck and trailer holding the yellow airplane from that fateful day sitting in the ranch driveway. She looked down at her hands, which were slowly starting to heal; she would have the scars to remember that day for the rest of her life.

"Let's get our horses put away," she told the group. As

saddles and blankets were pulled from horses, Elsie passed around curry combs to groom the animals. "I'll be back to check on you in a minute."

With her long braid bouncing at her back, she marched over to the truck and airplane. Suddenly, the peacefulness of the morning was gone and she felt her temper rising. Byron and Clay were standing and talking to two men in ball caps and heavily polarized sunglasses. As Elsie approached, all the men turned to look at her.

"This is the young lady to whom you truly owe the apology," Byron said. He was not smiling and Elsie could tell by the set of his mouth he was far from happy with the unexpected visitors.

The taller of the two men stepped forward; he wore leather boat shoes and tailored pants.

"I'm so sorry about the other day. I was just telling Mr. Ranvier that my sport plane was experiencing engine difficulty and I was looking for an alpine meadow in which to set her down. I should have kept away from the ranch, though, I am truly sorry for the danger I put you in. I hope you can accept my apology," the man with the boat shoes said. He removed his sunglasses and reached out to take Elsie's hand. "I'm Eric Marksmen."

Elsie looked at him. His eyes were clear, grayish blue with a few, fine laugh lines around at the corners. He had the look of someone who spent a lot of time outdoors.

"Elsie Rosewood," she said. "I honestly can't believe you didn't see all the horses and livestock we have here at the ranch and think to fly any other direction?" She held out her hand but kept her face expressionless.

"Oh, no. Did this happen because of me?" Eric said. He held her hand, palm up, and examined the healing rope burns.

Elsie snatched her hand away. "Yes, it did. Now excuse me, I have horses to see to."

"Wait, can I pay for your doctor bill?" Eric said. "Or buy you a pair of gloves?"

"No thanks," Elsie said. She marched toward the barn where she could see the two mothers and their daughters were nearly finished grooming the horses. She heard the airplane man running to catch up with her.

"Listen, I really am sorry. Could I take you to dinner to show you I'm not actually a bad guy who goes around trying to hurt people?"

Elsie did not know what to say. She stopped and turned to look at him, tucking the wisps of her long brown hair, which had pulled free from her braid, out of her eyes. He looked genuine and eager. She resisted the urge to turn on her heel and walk away from him. Instead, she looked him over. She noticed he had dimples when he flashed her a hesitant grin and the faint lines around his eyes were definitely from smiling.

"Look, I'm making a donation to the land trust behind the ranch so that I can show how sorry I really am. But I'd love to be able to take you to dinner and hear about the mustang you're training," Eric spoke quickly, as if he sensed she might walk away. "I've never met a girl who trains mustangs. Most of the woman I know back home go shopping or take up jogging for fun."

As Eric spoke, she suddenly saw Corbin in her mind's eye. The memory was from the grassy meadow where they had found Magic. She saw him sitting on his horse and watching her. She had expected to find mockery when she looked up to meet his gaze that evening, and instead, she found admiration. Her heart had stopped for a moment as she sensed a change in the man before her.

Eric was watching her and she realized she should say something. She wanted to be angry that a memory of Corbin came to her when a handsome man asked her out for dinner. She owed Corbin nothing, and for that matter, Eric was just being polite. She looked down at her boots. For the second time, the cloak of anger she had worn for so long was absent when she reached for its familiar warmth. She bit the inside of her cheek and realized she had to say yes, if for no other reason than she had pictured Corbin Darkhorse. Somehow, her errant imagination was lolling her into believing she could trust a man who had left her when she needed him most. Unsettled, she pushed that thought away. Right now, she had no time to ponder her own fickle attraction to Corbin.

"Okay. I'm off Friday," Elsie said.

"Great! I'll come and pick you up around seven, does that work?" Eric said.

"Yes," Elsie said. It might actually be nice to get away from the ranch for an evening and not have to think about the competition or Corbin.

"'Til Friday, Elsie," Eric said. He was staring again and Elsie looked down. She felt her face beginning to flush. This handsome stranger was flirting with her.

Corbin came riding in, with fence repair snips and extra wire hanging from his saddle, just as the airplane men pulled out of the driveway. Elsie did her best to ignore him and so bent down to retie a piece of loose fringe on her chaps.

"Is that the jerk who almost killed Elsie?" Corbin said.

"Yep, that's also the guy who's taking Elsie on a date Friday night and just donated $5,000 to the land trust behind us," Clay said.

"You took money from them?" Corbin's irritation was evident.

"Calm down, Corbin," Byron said. "They were having engine trouble, and we could hardly turn down $5,000 to maintain the trails and cut fire paths."

"It's not about the money." Corbin's words were heavy with sarcasm.

"Maybe you should ask Elsie on a date if it bugs you that much," Clay said.

"It doesn't 'bug' me," Corbin replied. "I just think it's wrong for him to ask her to go on a date with him."

"Why is that?" Byron said. He pulled a burr from Nighthawk's mane and then patted the horse's damp neck.

"Because he's good-looking and rich?"

"No," Corbin answered. "He just shouldn't have come back here after almost getting her seriously hurt."

Elsie kept her head down as she walked away. Suddenly, the morning seemed less peaceful.

"As I remember it," Clay chimed in. "You managed to save the day so it worked out just fine."

Elsie felt a smile pulling at her lips. She glanced back to see that Corbin did look very annoyed.

Elsie was adding supplements to the horses' feed buckets when Corbin entered the tack room only a few minutes later.

"What are you thinking, going to dinner with that idiot in the plane?" he asked.

"It's just dinner." Elsie kept her voice even.

"He about killed you! Who knows what dinner might lead to—crash landing in a supermarket?"

"It's no big deal." She knew this was not entirely true and she was starting to get excited. It had been so long since she'd been on any type of date. Seeing Corbin upset suddenly made Eric seem so sincere. Maybe Eric was not handsome in the same dark and stunning way that Corbin was, but Corbin was difficult, untrustworthy, mouthy, flirtatious, annoying, and cocky. The list could go on and on. She wished she didn't notice that he sat his horse as if he were more centaur than man.

"I don't think you should go." Corbin's statement pulled her back to the present.

Elsie stopped mixing the feed and looked up at him. "Let's get one thing straight, you can't tell me what to do. In fact, why don't you just turn around and walk out of here and not talk to me until we practice for our next performance?"

Corbin kicked the door open and strode out. He turned back at the entrance to the barn and said, "You're so damn stubborn, I hope you go on that date and have a great time. In fact, I hope you have such a great time you spend all your days with that rich, airplane asshole. But don't come crying to me when that mustang of yours is still as wild as the day you picked him up."

"How dare you!" Elsie said. She set down the feed scoop and followed Corbin out of the barn. "I think I deserve one night of a little fun. You take time off whenever you want. Just because I'm actually trying to build a relationship with my mustang and not just 'break it' like you are, doesn't mean that I won't win at the competition. How dare you have the nerve to tell me I'm going to lose?"

"Keep it down, you two. We have guests," Lenora said. The other woman appeared by the tack room door.

Corbin shook his head and walked out to the cow barn. Elsie stood with Lenora and watched him go.

"Sorry," Elsie said. "I don't know how he gets under my skin so easily."

"You two are a lot alike. Sometimes that will do it," Lenora answered. "You know, he's not used to girls turning him down."

"He left me when I needed him most." More hurt than she wanted to share with her hostess spilled forth, making her regret her words as soon as they left her mouth.

"The accident?" Lenora said.

"Yes." Elsie loaded a bale of hay into the wheelbarrow, hoping Lenora would give up and go back in the house.

"I went to the library and dug up the old article in the archives," Lenora continued. "After I knew you were coming to work for us. I think you're brave for training a mustang again.

"They put down the horse that trampled me." Elsie found herself speaking almost against her will. "It was never her fault. She was just a wild mare and they pushed us to get them broke in a day. It's too much for a lot of horses to take in. That poor horse was just scared and trying to run."

"Still, I think you're brave," Lenora said. She grabbed another bale of hay from the stack. "And I see how much time you take with Magic. You're giving him all the respect and space he needs to be able to figure out humans."

Elsie pushed the wheelbarrow out to the paddock and Lenora cut the twine holding the bales together. The women grabbed flakes of the second-cutting alfalfa and threw them over the fence to the waiting horses.

"I don't know why Corbin left you in the hospital," Lenora said. "But I see he regrets it every day."

"I'm not sure about that," Elsie said. But then she thought back to the impromptu camping trip and their intense night of near-passion. Somehow, they had both been trying to figure out where the boundaries lay between them. The past had been a looming chasm, darker and wider than either had realized.

"I guess I just think Corbin would like us all to believe that he's as tough and full of himself as he pretends to be. But I know underneath all of that he has a big heart. Maybe that scares him?" Lenora spoke slowly and Elsie had the feeling the older woman had put some thought into her words. "He wouldn't be the first guy to try and hide his soft spots from the world. You should ask Clay about their father. From what I hear, things were harder on Corbin than Clay, when it came to their dad."

Elsie was quiet. The last thing she wanted was to argue with the woman who had so graciously taken her in, but the idea of delving into what idiotic excuse Corbin had for walking out on her when she needed him most was not appealing in the least.

Lenora sensed Elsie's hesitation and hurriedly continued. "I guess it sounds like I'm taking Corbin's side and I'm not." She paused and kissed the gray and pink nose of her white Arabian horse, Major Temptation. The gelding rested his head on Lenora's chest. "I haven't been riding him as much lately." She ran her hand over her belly. "But I think he knows there's a baby in here because he is so gentle and careful with me when we do go up to the mountains."

Elsie silently berated herself for doubting Lenora's genuine interest in her situation with Corbin. The older woman obviously wanted the best for Elsie. "Does it feel funny?" Elsie asked. "To ride?"

"A little. My balance is off but at least right now I still love being in the saddle."

Major snuffled Lenora's hair before going back to his flake of hay.

"I can't imagine," Elsie said. "I've never really thought about having a child. I've been fighting so hard to ride and train horses again I guess I just haven't really ever thought before…" She trailed off.

"Oh I understand," Lenora said. "Believe me, I am very shocked to find myself married again and now pregnant. It's beautiful how we change as we go through life. Keeps it interesting, you know?"

"I guess you're right. But sometimes I'm scared of what's in store for me next."

"Oh, believe me; I was like that for a long time after my mother passed away. I just felt like I couldn't trust life not to destroy me completely." Lenora waved toward the mountains. "But when I did start to trust life again, I found it to be sweeter the second time around."

The two women headed back toward the barn, Elsie pushing the hay cart as she mulled Lenora's words around in her head. When was the last time she had trusted everything would turn out all right? So long ago that she couldn't even remember what that felt like. Her whole body was drawn tight and ready for the next struggle. She took a deep breath as they walked in silence.

"Let me know if you want any help getting ready for your date." Lenora spoke quietly as if she felt that Elsie was still contemplating their earlier conversation. "Or maybe you'd like to borrow a dress?"

"Actually, that would really amazing. I don't have

anything to wear except jeans and boots. I wasn't really thinking it was a date but everyone else keeps calling it that, so I guess I better dress up a little," Elsie said.

"Well, whatever it is, it doesn't hurt to wear a dress and some makeup," Lenora said. "If for no other reason than it's great to get fancied up from time to time! Especially when you live on a ranch in the middle of nowhere." She shot Elsie a mischievous look in the fading light. "Did Rosa tell you that she and I met when I bought lingerie at her shop?"

"No, she definitely did not."

"We'll tell you that story someday over a couple of drinks."

CHAPTER NINE

Corbin was waiting outside the round pen at six AM the next morning.

"I'm calling in my favor now. I want to know how you're teaching Magic to lie down."

He was wearing a plain, white T-shirt and his hair was still messy from sleep. A strange mix of determination and anger warred on his face. Elsie stood still, her hand resting on the doorknob of her horse trailer. Her first urge was to ignore him and walk away. How dare he show up during the early morning time she reserved for training her mustang and expect her to drop everything? He stared at her, his eyes challenging her to say something, anything. She squared her shoulders and then deliberately closed the door to her horse trailer. It was too early in the morning to be this angry and she tried to calm herself. She knew this had little to do with horse training and much to do with her impending date with the airplane man.

When she turned back toward Corbin, her voice was cool and polite. "Let me be very clear with you. This is my space, my time to train my horse. You can't just show up whenever you..." Her voice was rising in pitch. She forced herself to stop and take a breath. She couldn't look at him, he made her so mad. It especially didn't help that his skin was still damp from a shower and the morning sun was making him glisten. He never did up the last buttons on his shirt and now she was imagining the way her fingers would play across his chest. She stopped herself, turned away, angry and frustrated and wanting to hop on the nearest horse and ride like hell for the mountains. Why did he have to stir up such a war of desire and anger inside her rapidly beating heart?

"You were saying?" Corbin interrupted her thoughts and snapped her back into the reality of the situation.

"This is my time." She had to stand her ground with this man.

There was a long pause and Corbin looked down. He moved over to the fence and then looked back at her. She had expected a grin, the cocky, I'm-a-fancy-horse-trainer smile that was plastered on the side of his truck and horse trailer. Instead, his brows pulled together and she could see that he wanted to ask her a question. He must have thought better of it and looked at the mustang watching them. "I was impressed with the way you caught him in the valley," he said simply. "Perhaps another time?"

He looked vulnerable and boyish. He ran a hand absently through his hair. She took a deep breath.

"Fine. Let's get this over with right now," Elsie said. She entered the corral and Magic nickered to her. He trotted over and rested his head against her shoulder. "I know you think there's some amazing secret, but really it's just about trust, timing, and release—like everything else in training horses."

With her hand, she directed Magic away from her and then as soon as he sniffed the ground, she gave him a treat. The mustang looked happy and sniffed the ground again. Each time he offered the behavior Elsie wanted, she rewarded him.

"Now, I just have to teach the cue," Elsie said. "Then he'll lie down whenever I want him to."

This time she used a long whip and tickled his front leg. Once he looked down and lowered his neck, she stopped. After five minutes of repetition, Magic was sniffing the ground on cue and then bending his front legs, the way that horses do when they are about to lie down. After another five minutes, the mustang lay down with a sigh. Elsie rubbed her hands along his neck and gave him two slices of apple.

Corbin let out a low whistle of appreciation.

When she glanced back at him leaning against the corral rail, his eyebrows were drawn together and something almost wistful lingered in his eyes.

"Thanks, Elsie. Guess I better get started with my big gray. You have fun on Friday with that crazy airplane man," Corbin said. He pushed away from the panels of the round pen and headed back toward the barn.

Nearly out of earshot, he said, "Just be careful, okay?"

Her stomach clenched and for a moment she wanted to call after him. Her voice caught in her throat when she realized she had no idea what she would say.

***

Corbin wanted to kick something, preferably his own ass. Each time he thought he was making a little headway with Elsie, he was met with her stubborn refusal to see beyond who he used to be. He didn't entirely blame her. Still, it would be so much easier if she would just give him a chance. He walked past his horse trailer and couldn't bring himself to look at his smiling, larger-than-life face plastered on the side. No wonder she was not going to give him a second chance. He strongly doubted he would give himself a second chance if he were in her place.

The sun was warm on his shoulders and he whistled for the gray. The big horse raised his head from the green pasture and looked at Corbin. With his ears perked forward and wind ruffling his mane, he looked pretty spectacular, a true American treasure. It was hard to believe that so many people thought these wild and beautiful horses were disposable trash. Corbin took a deep breath and tried to relax his tensed jaw. The mustang took a few tentative steps toward Corbin. He climbed over the fence and stood with his arms hanging loose at his sides. The horse took a few more steps toward him. Patience was not his strong suit, he knew this. His mother had often sent him outside to sit on a rock warmed in the sun and watch for red-tailed hawks in the sky. "Keep looking," she would say when he ran back into the house to advise her that there were no birds in the sky. He often wondered how she had been able to raise two boys as wild and strong-willed as he and Clay, but he knew now she'd had her ways of teaching them. Maybe he should have paid more attention.

The horse kept coming. Corbin rested his hand on the gray's withers when the animal finally stopped. He felt a slow grin spread across his face. Maybe, just maybe, he actually stood a chance at giving Elsie some competition. He ran his hands over the horse's back, luxuriating in the animal's silky summer coat. The wind kicked up a little and the gray raised his head. Corbin spoke softly, reassuring the horse. With his right hand, he grabbed a handful of the horse's mane, ran his left hand over the animal's shoulder, and then rocked back on his outside leg. He swung himself up onto the horse's back, landing so softly the horse barely flicked an ear back.

Corbin sat on the horse and watched as Byron and Clay walked toward him. They stopped at the fence.

"Rough night or bad morning?" Byron said in way of hello.

"Neither." Corbin did not want to elaborate.

"Well, that's something." Clay watched his brother as he spoke. "How about finishing up the north fence line?"

"Of course," Corbin replied. He slid off the mustang and headed toward the ranch truck.

"I'll keep you company," Clay said as Corbin walked away. Last year, the two brothers had stretched a new line of fence enabling the use of the North Pasture during the dry season. They hadn't quite finished the job.

Corbin grimaced and kept his head down. He needed to find his hat.

"Don't have too much fun up there," Byron said. "I'll get some food packed up while the both of you load that truck."

Corbin knew they'd been talking about him. He didn't share the close bond with Byron that Clay did. In fact, he often had the feeling that the older man was watching him and waiting for him to mess up. He imagined they had been less than charitable during their discussion.

In complete silence, the two men loaded posts in the back of the truck. The sun was high overhead and a light breeze blew down from the westernmost peaks.

Finally, once the posts were loaded and arranged to Clay's liking, he spoke. "You're acting like a damn, stubborn fool."

Corbin didn't give his brother the satisfaction of agreeing with him. Instead, he tossed rolls of wire onto the bed of the pickup truck. "Let's go," he said.

Byron handed over a canvas bag with food and a small cooler. They stopped the truck next to Corbin's quarters, long enough for him to grab a jacket for the evening and a change of clothes. By the time they finished, it would be dark and the road home was barely more than a dirt track.

***

The road turned from gravel to dirt as they headed through the meadows and into the bowl, which spanned wide from ridge to ridge and was filled with Indian Paintbrush. The mountains reached down, heavily cloaked in red pine and spruce. Corbin felt his spirits rise as they moved away from the ranch.

Without speaking, Clay stopped the truck and let Corbin out. The fence stretched away under the tree line to the east and west. Corbin grabbed some tools and then watched his brother drive further along the line of crooked and leaning fence posts. They would work in solitude for a while, for this Corbin was grateful. As his body fell into the routine of stretching wire and digging post holes, his mind eased into a rhythm of contemplation—a day of seclusion in God's country was what he needed.

***

Later, they jounced along the rutted drive leading to the back pasture. The light was turning heavy-gold as the sun rested on the shoulders of Bear Peak. Corbin ran his tongue over his teeth and tried to think of something besides, *you're right*, to say to his brother. An especially deep rut threw Corbin so that he had to brace his hand on the dash or get propelled through it.

"Would you slow down?" His voice had more of an irritable edge than he had intended.

"Are you gonna talk?" Clay replied. His voice was heavy with older-brother-knows-best.

"Sure. What do you want to talk about?" Corbin said. He knew his slow drawl and feigned ignorance would drive his brother crazy.

Clay slammed on the brakes. "You're starting to remind me of Dad," he said.

Corbin ignored he low jab.

"Seriously," Clay said. "You've gotten a pretty good start on his lifestyle."

Corbin felt a sick knot start to form in the pit of his stomach. He wanted to hit something or someone, maybe Clay.

"I'm nothing like him," Corbin managed to spit out.

"Really?" Clay spoke slowly.

"You're one to talk," Corbin said. "How about we ask

your ex-wife how she feels?"

He knew that was a too much even as the words left his lips. He wished he could take them back but they now lay between the two men and were spreading like fog in the valley. Clay cut the engine and slammed the truck door as he climbed out. Corbin followed him. They stood and watched each other, their shoulders squared and backs stiff.

Then Clay started to laugh. Corbin stared.

Clay came around the truck and clasped Corbin's shoulders. For a long minute, the two men held each other and then the sun sank the last bit behind the mountain and they separated. The bond of siblings held strong. They both understood the other in a way no human alive could, not even their mother. Their formative years growing up had been so identical, and even though they turned out to be different people, with different dreams and lives, they now found themselves thrown back together. Clay's injury last year had forced them into working proximity with each other. Now nearly eighteen months later, they were suddenly both very aware that they were bonded brothers and yet unsettled with their unspoken past.

Clay spoke first. "The way I see it. We have two choices: follow in Dad's steps or forge our own new path."

"I agree," Corbin said. He folded his arms across his chest. With the toe of his boot, he nudged the top of a rock buried in the earth. "Sometimes I feel like his legacy has fallen to me."

"Why?" Clay replied. His face was surprised and Corbin watched his brother's eyes.

"Because you so neatly sidestepped it," Corbin said. "Is it possible for both of us to avoid being like that old cheating, swindling cowboy?"

"Of course, it is," Clay said. "Look, the last thing I want is to see you wandering around the country turning into someone who believes his own brand of lies. You're good with horses, real good. But you also have a solid heart, a curious mind, and a strong will to do right. I see it in you."

"Sometimes I think it would just be easier," Corbin said. "You know? To just drive around with my rig and give clinics and talk to all the pretty, rich women, take their money and warm their beds for as long as I like. Then move on."

"Of course, it's easier," Clay said. "Why do you think Dad chose that path for so long?"

"But it gets pretty lonely when you can no longer feel the truth. The problem with lying to yourself is that, eventually, you have to either completely believe the lies or else have a painful day of reckoning. Remember that you and I will always walk closer to the earth than he did. It's a great gift but also means great pain if we turn away from our true path and lose ourselves in the world we now live in."

Corbin was silent. So many times before when his brother talked about their heritage and time living on the reservation he became embarrassed and angry. Ironic, he thought, because he knew his Lakota blood made all the wealthy horsewomen want him even more. Somehow being Native American made so many people trust his advice with their horses and buy into his stories.

The men climbed back into the truck and began to drive. The shadows had joined forces and the whole valley was dark. As they crested a small rise, the creek to the east caught a little of the faded rays of the sun and the water turned orange and fire-red.

"I know," Corbin said after they had both been silent for nearly twenty minutes. "That he wasn't happy with the life he chose. And I don't think I would be either."

Clay kept his eyes on the dirt track as they descended the other side of the rise. The small fence-line cabin came into view, its weathered pine logs bleached nearly white in some places. "There's a kind of joy," he said. "Knowing you've married to the woman you'll grow old with, it's so much deeper than I ever imagined."

"Is it like with a well-broke horse?" Corbin said. "The way you get a partnership going and you read each other? A trust that goes far beyond the current moment?"

Clay laughed. "There's nothing 'well-broke' about Lenora, and I imagine Elsie won't take too well to being spurred either, but you're right about the partnership. And the trust, too."

Corbin mulled over the last word. Being trustworthy was something all horses liked in their humans. He knew this and yet it seemed like for a long time, he had done everything but be trustworthy. Now he was paying the price for his actions.

They pulled up beside the cabin and got out of the truck. The sound of rushing water reached their ears from the creek just down the slight hill. Corbin rolled his shoulders and ran his hand over the back of his neck. "Cold dip before dinner?"

"Let's get the fire going first." Clay flashed a quick smile at his brother.

"Getting old and soft, huh?"

"Just wise."

Corbin headed off to gather kindling from the lodgepole pines behind the cabin while Clay carried their few belongings into the cabin. Once they had a good fire going, they headed down to the creek. A large granite boulder, still a little warm from the sun, stuck out into the fast-moving water. The pool of relatively calm water, about shoulder-deep for the men, eddied around the base of the pinkish stone. Corbin stripped down quickly and then Clay followed, saving his boots for nearly last. Corbin leaped in, shouting as he surfaced in the frigid water. "Colder than last year," he announced.

Clay followed him in. "Damn, you're right," he said, pulling his black hair from his eyes.

Corbin grinned at his brother, water beading on his eyelashes.

"What?" Clay eyed him with distrust.

"You're going to be a dad." Corbin was still smiling.

"I am." A softness crept over Clay's features.

"A really good dad." Corbin grabbed his brother's shoulders and dunked him.

When Clay surfaced, they wrestled around in the shallows for a few moments before scrambling out of the icy mountain stream.

As they walked back to the cabin, their skin tingling from the chill water, Corbin felt a glow of joy. He knew he was beyond lucky to be with his brother again. The two of them fought sometimes, and Clay had the most annoying habit of acting like he had it all figured out, but still, to be able to spend time in the mountains with his brother was a true luxury. Silently, he found himself sending up a prayer of thanks.

Much later, the firelight filling the tiny cabin, both men in their bedrolls, Clay spoke. "I'm scared this time around." His voice was low.

Corbin rolled over and looked at his brother. Clay stared into the fire, his eyes lost in shadow.

"It will be different." Corbin hoped his words offered some measure of assurance.

"I know it will," Clay said. "I can feel it. But, sometimes, at night, I wake up and roll over in bed and look at her sleeping and just pray and pray that God will keep her and the baby safe."

A log shifted in the fireplace and a shower of sparks shot up. What could he say? Corbin wondered. For a small moment, he imagined what it might be like to have a child with Elsie. What if that baby died? He felt his whole heart constrict. His brother had been through so much. Carefully, he chose his words. "This time is different, everything about it is new. Remember how Mom used to send us out at sunrise every day we weren't in school? She would tell us to be brave and go have a grand adventure?"

He paused, staring into the fire and trying to find the right words. "I think you just have to live every day with Lenora and your growing family just like that—a beautiful, grand adventure. Of course that takes bravery and a good measure of trust."

"You know she just wanted us out of the house so she could paint, right?" Clay's white teeth flashed in the firelight as he spoke.

"Of course. We drove Mom crazy but I think she taught us how to treat each day with a special respect. But," he added, "I forget all the time."

"Yeah, me too."

They fell silent. The fire popped and outside a lone coyote howled from the ridge to the north behind the cabin.

"I'm very proud of you." Corbin spoke slowly. "For being brave enough to try again."

Clay turned toward him, his face half in shadow.

"I have to. What's the other choice? To quit? To walk away? I'd risk anything for a chance at having a family with Lenora." Clay stared into the fire. "But it really terrifies me." He paused and Corbin could tell he was weighing his words carefully before he spoke again. "I think you're going to have to really apologize to Elsie. Put yourself fully out there."

Corbin started to speak and Clay cut him off. "I know you think I'm just a pushy big brother, but I think you haven't really apologized to her. She's hurt and she has every right to feel that way, but if you can be truly vulnerable and honest with her, you might have a chance to win back her trust."

Corbin felt the old anger rise in his chest and it mingled with a heavy dose of shame. He took a deep breath. Very easily, he could fight with Clay, storm out of the cabin, and then drink some whiskey alone under the stars. He had done that before when he found Clay's advice too patronizing. But as he took another deep breath, he decided to try something new; he would wait. One thing he had learned, when he finally stopped running after Elsie's accident, was that leaving never made the shame diminish or the anger ease.

"She won't acknowledge my apology. I've tried."

"You are going to have to keep trying. A girl as tough, sexy, and intelligent as Elsie will never come your way again."

"I know," Corbin said. "We're a good fit. I still remember the first day I saw her sitting on that big chestnut gelding. I knew that I had to talk to her no matter what but then somehow I messed everything up and got her hurt."

"You can't control horses, you know that." Clay sat up on his bedroll.

"I know, but Elsie wasn't even keen on the whole competition. She kept saying that it was too fast to start a horse, but I pushed because I loved the crowd and the excitement and the way people looked at me when I worked with a really wild horse." Corbin paused but kept his eyes on the fire. The shame in his stomach was hot and stirred around uncomfortably. "I think back on it and I just want to punch my younger self in the gut."

"Hey, easy now." Clay grabbed Corbin's arm. "There's no going back and redoing the past. All I'm saying is let her know how sorry you truly are. Do what Dad never could do, and really say you're sorry and then back up your words with actions. I don't know if she'll forgive you, but that's up to her." Clay released his brother's arm. "Just do your part and make amends."

The coyote howled again and then another answered from across the ridge. Corbin could hear the wind picking up outside the cabin. It brought the scent of rain from the west.

Corbin was almost asleep when Clay shifted on his bedroll. The fire had burnt low and his whole body was warm and relaxed.

"Having you at Bear Dance Ranch has been the best gift I could've ever asked for."

Corbin smiled and let sleep drift over his mind like a soft mist.

CHRISTINA RHOADS

CHAPTER TEN

At six PM, with chores and a long day behind her, Elsie climbed the stairs to Lenora and Clay's room.

"Take a nice long shower. I'll be up as soon as this quiche is ready to pop in the oven," Lenora said. "We can go over which dress you would like to wear."

Elsie took off her dirty work jeans and shirt and took a long shower. She had forgotten how nice it was to have unlimited amounts of hot water and she found herself humming an old Patsy Cline tune.

Lenora had three dresses laid out on the bed: a red one with a high waist and low back, a black one with a short hemline, and the last was cream-colored with an overlay of delicate lace. Elsie swallowed, suddenly feeling intimidated. She was going on a date with a man she didn't even know.

Lenora knocked at the bedroom door. As if sensing Elsie's unease, she spoke softly. "I think you better try each of them on. Just see how they feel."

Elsie ran her hand over the satin fabric of the red dress. How long had it been since she had gone out for fun with someone interesting? Her mind kept pulling up a blank. After the accident, her life had been filled with surgeries and then rehab. Almost three years of stretching and

115

strengthening and then learning to walk again without aid. Her body had to adjust to a rod where a large section of her femur had once been, as well as the numerous screws, pins, and plates that allowed her to walk again. Once she was finally able to ride, she had always felt like she was playing catchup to the other horse trainers. She had apprenticed to some of the most respected horsemen and women and tried to learn as much as she could. There had never been time for dating. Sure, she had let a few cowboys buy her drinks, but she had never allowed it lead to anything more.

"Long time since you've been on a date?" Lenora smoothed her hand over the lacey dress.

"Years and years." Elsie grimaced.

"I understand. Before Clay, it had been a few years for me too." She laughed. "We were both so awkward with each other. I seriously thought he didn't even notice me."

"And now you're having a baby together."

"We are. It's hard to believe sometimes." Lenora looked down at her growing midsection and ran her hand over the bump. "Just remember this is for fun. You deserve a night away from the ranch. Don't put too much pressure on the situation. The guy might end up being really boring or rude."

Elsie smiled; this was like getting ready with her sisters. There had been a few dances in high school when they helped her with her hair and all shared clothes and lipstick tubes. Elsie dropped her robe and tried on the dresses. As soon as she put on the cream one, she knew it was right.

"Oh, yes. That's the one," Lenora said in agreement when Elsie came out on the landing to show her. "You could wear your good turquoise cowboy boots and then you won't look too dressy if he takes you to the Painted Pony."

"Perfect, I don't want to feel uncomfortable all night either. This is so me," Elsie said. She looked down and touched the cream-colored lace. The vintage style was perfect. Plus, she reasoned, her limp was less pronounced in cowboy boots.

"Can I curl your hair?" Lenora asked. "I bet it will look just perfect with big, loose waves."

"Yes, I'd love that." Elsie ran her hand over her long hair. It felt so nice to be pampered a little.

"You know I never had any siblings?" Lenora said. "I always dreamed about having a sister." She sat Elsie down in front of the vanity and brushed her long, brown hair until it was smooth and rippling in the light. Then she brandished the curling iron and made heavy, full waves that hung around Elsie's face and down her back.

"I have two sisters. But we aren't that close." Elsie hesitated, realizing that she had never returned a missed call from Hazel a week or more back. "That's sort of my fault."

"Family is tricky." Lenora was efficient as she twisted Elsie's long hair. "But it's good to always remember what you have in common, and not the differences that separate you. Just my opinion, of course." Lenora laughed. "Easy for me to forgive siblings I don't have!"

"You're right." Elsie smiled at Lenora in the mirror. The other woman looked so beautiful, her skin glowing in the late afternoon light and hair a golden, rust hallow around her face. If she were to pick a sister, Elsie thought, she would want one just like Lenora. "I've spent nearly a decade trying to prove to everyone that I can still train horses and compete with the best in this country."

"It must have been so scary," Lenora said. "To think you might never again do what you love?"

"Yes, it was." Elsie touched a soft curl that Lenora had just formed. "I should call my sisters though. I can't get so caught up in trying to win."

"I bet they'd like to hear from you."

There was a long silence and Elsie closed her eyes for a moment. The butterflies in her stomach had subsided a little. Lenora's hands were soothing and she felt her shoulders unclench.

"Annie said that you and Clay are waiting to learn the baby's gender?"

"We are. It's strange, but we just want it to be a surprise." Lenora met Elsie's eyes in the mirror. "We weren't sure that we could get pregnant when we first started trying and Clay had so much fear." She looked down running the brush through the loose waves in Elsie's hair.

"He lost his baby? There was a fever?"

"Yes." Lenora twisted the last few locks of Elsie's hair around the curling iron. "He's still hurting from that loss."

"I sort of remember. Corbin and I were headed to a show when their mother called."

"Really? It's so strange to think of you and Corbin together back then."

"It was a terrible mistake." Elsie knew her voice was flat and angry.

"I'm sorry. It must have hurt." Lenora misted Elsie's hair with setting spray. "I mean, the surgeries and rehabs and all the hard work that it took to ride again.

"Yes." Elsie tried to keep her tone neutral. The past had a slithering way of ruining the present, and right now, she didn't want to think about Corbin. She met Lenora's eyes in the mirror and saw so much compassion in the other woman's face that she had to quickly duck her head. She didn't need anyone to pity her.

"Perfect." Lenora was brusque again and smiled as she ran her hand through Elsie's long soft waves of hair.

"Wow. Thanks," Elsie said. She felt a little shy as she looked at her reflection. It had been so long since she had looked in the mirror and liked what she saw. So much of the last ten years had been a struggle to regain her ability to walk, ride, and train horses. It felt as if she had somehow missed out on the whole going-on-dates-and-looking-pretty thing, and until this moment, she didn't even know she wanted any of it.

Downstairs, Lenora opened the front door and then paused. "The boys must have made it back from their fence-fixing party," Lenora said. "Because they're both leaning against the porch rail."

"Really?" A knot formed in Elsie's stomach.

"Looks like Corbin's trying to play it cool." Lenora opened the door all the way and turned back to give Elsie a quick smile. "Those guys aren't going to believe how beautiful you look."

Elsie felt herself blush; she wasn't used to being the center of attention. She took a deep breath and stepped out onto the porch.

The sun was just hovering at the tip of the mountains to the west and the last golden rays caught in her eyes. Standing by a Jeep, with fancy lights and an off-road bumper and winch, was Eric. Byron stood next to him and the two were talking. Everyone turned and stared as Elsie took the two steps down to the gravel drive and walked toward Eric and Byron.

"Hey, Elsie, you look great," Clay called.

Elsie turned and smiled. Clay put his arm around Lenora. His brother stood next to him. For just a moment, she allowed herself to meet Corbin's eyes. The look of sheer anger made her hesitate for a moment.

Corbin swung his leg over the porch rail and was next to Elsie in a moment. He stood too close and stared down at her before speaking.

"What are you thinking, going out with this clown?" He cupped her elbow with the palm of his hand, his fingers barely brushing her skin.

"Excuse me, but he's standing right behind us," Elsie said. "And you're making a scene."

"Please don't go out looking like that." His eyes were locked with hers and she had to look down in order to breathe. She could not believe her heart was beating this fast over Corbin Darkhorse. She reminded herself that this was the man who had abandoned her after her accident. He was also a known womanizer and the one person standing in her way to winning the Mustang Competition.

"Is there a problem?" Eric said.

"No, not at all," Elsie answered. "Corbin was just letting go of my arm."

"I can't believe you have the nerve to come to this ranch and try to buy your way out of what you did," Corbin said. His fingers still rested on Elsie's arm. "You came very near to getting her killed."

"Look," Eric said. "I'm very sorry. Like I told Elsie, and also Mr. Ranvier, I'm trying to be a decent human being and apologize."

"Well, that better be all you do," Corbin said. "I hope you understand me when I tell she has family here at Bear Dance, and we won't stand to see her mishandled in *any* way."

"Of course not," Eric said. He had his hands out in a friendly way, but Elsie saw the hint of a temper below the surface of his smooth smile. "Is there something going on here that I'm getting in the middle of?"

"No," Elsie said. She glared at Corbin and jerked her arm, with more force than was necessary, from his feather-touch grasp.

Corbin said nothing but instead stood and clenched his jaw before crossing his arms across his chest.

"Let's go," Elsie said to Eric.

Eric placed his hand on the small of her back. He politely steered her toward his Jeep and opened the door for her.

"Have a great time," Lenora called from the porch.

As they pulled away, Elsie glanced in the side mirror to see Corbin stalking off to the barn. Her own temper flared for a moment as she remembered lying in the hospital bed, wondering if he would come to see her that day. There had been a long string of days like that before she realized he was never coming back.

She leaned back in the seat; never again, she promised herself, would she let that man get under her skin.

Turning to Eric, she said, "I'm so sorry about that. Corbin is so competitive, he can't stand the idea of anything getting in the way of the Mustang Competition."

"It's no big deal. But I think he might have a thing for you." He looked away from the road to give her a smile. His eyes were very blue, she noticed, and clear.

"I doubt it, he has so many girls after him," Elsie replied. "But enough about that! I'm excited to know where we're going." In an attempt to ease the previous awkwardness at the ranch, she found herself putting on a somewhat forced bubbly demeanor.

"Ahh, it's a surprise," he said. He looked away from the mountain road again and winked. "I do hope you know that I still feel terrible about scaring your mustang and getting you hurt."

"I'm fine, really. I guess you're lucky you didn't crash your plane," Elsie said.

"Well, it wouldn't be the first time." He grinned and she imagined he was reliving a hairy aerial situation.

"Really? You've crashed before?"

"When you have a thing for antique planes, you have to realize that the risk of making unexpected landings is pretty high," Eric said. "It's in my blood. Both of my grandfathers flew in the British Air Force, during World War II."

"Really? I don't detect an accent," Elsie said.

"Oh, it's long gone. I've been in the States for most of my life."

The rest of the drive flew by as Eric told her about life back in England and tried to explain his passion for antique planes. When they finally stopped on the square, in Lakeside, Elsie was surprised at how easily the conversation had begun to flow between them. Eric opened the door and offered her his arm. He steered them toward a tiny brick restaurant with flower boxes on the windows and green shutters. Inside, the hostess greeted Eric by his first name and then led the way to a nook where a small table overlooked the garden outside. Beyond the restaurant was the edge of Flathead Lake.

As Elsie sat down, she thought, for the briefest of moments, how nice it would be if Corbin could act this way and take her to a nice restaurant. Perhaps, she could forgive him if he tried a little more. The only time she had not been mad at that frustrating man was on their single-night truce and that had led to a dangerously close call with sex. She looked up and found Eric's clear blue eyes on her.

"You look absolutely beautiful tonight, Elsie." Eric smiled, almost shyly, and his eyes were admiring. "Thanks for letting me take you to dinner."

"Thanks for asking me," Elsie said. She told herself to put Corbin and the competition out of her mind for one night.

"So you're training this wild mustang?"

"Yes. It's been a goal of mine for a long time." Elsie hesitated. The wine was going to her head. "I was thrown from a mustang and then trampled a long time ago." Her hand rested on the hemline of her dress; she could feel the raised scar running nearly the length of her thigh.

"I thought you had a limp. It's a little sexy." Eric laughed. "That sounded weird." He blushed under his tan and Elsie found herself liking his boyish eagerness. "What I meant," he continued hurriedly, "is that it lends you a little mystery."

Elsie smiled and felt herself flush as well. Eric Marksman found her sexy. It was nice to be admired, nice to feel like she was desirable and pretty.

"So now you have a certain number of days to get this horse ready for a competition?"

"Yes. Basically, I have one hundred days to get my mustang broke to ride and trained to compete at the Mustang Challenge. A group of horsewomen and men all put in applications to be able to compete against each other for the title of Mustang Champion and also a jackpot of $100,000."

"I see. Well, it's an honor to even be chosen." He raised his glass and clinked it against hers.

"This is also a calling for me. So many of the wild horses never get a fair chance. They're rounded up from their home in the mountains or steppes, sorted according to age and sex and separated from their families forever. Horses, kind of like us humans, form strong social bonds and it's heartbreaking to see them separated from their herd." She paused, knowing she had probably gone too far but unable to stop. "I hate it."

"So what will you do with your mustang?" Eric was intent upon her face as he spoke.

"I want to be an ambassador for the wild horse, you know? Let people understand what's going on. So many of the mustangs end up being sold by the pound for meat and shipped across the border to Canada or down to Mexico, for a very grizzly end.

"That's terrible."

"It is. Did you know that Congress has only ever passed a bill to protect two animals, ever? That's it, two animals, all the rest is decided by individual states. Guess which two?"

"The bald eagle, of course."

"And the American Mustang," Elsie jumped in then laughed. "Sorry, I'm a little passionate about this topic, as you can tell."

"I love passion. I come from a long line of very determined people but I'm not sure that any of them were as passionate as you are." He held her eyes as he spoke. "So why do so many of the mustangs end up being used for meat?"

Elsie leaned back in her chair. "A whole list of complex reasons: but basically the government owns a lot of wild horses and they don't know what to do with them.

Sometimes they turn a blind eye, when a man with a big truck, offers to buy four or five thousand mustangs. Part of the problem is that the horses are reproducing quickly, without many natural predators to keep their numbers in check. There's also a lot of push by the cattle people to allow more cows than mustangs on the federal land. Plus not many people have the skills to adopt and train a wild horse. They can be dangerous."

"As you've experienced."

"Yes."

"But this time is different?" Eric's eyes turned a darker blue, more like the sky at dusk.

"It is, and I'm going to win."

Eric raised his eyebrows slightly. "Elsie, I've only known you for about two and half hours and I am completely convinced that you will. I've never met a girl like you. Ever."

Elsie smiled and ran her finger along the damp edge of her wine glass. She realized, not for the first time, that any man she ended up with would have to be strong enough to match her fire.

After dinner, they strolled through downtown to the edge of the lake. Night had settled quietly over the town. To the west along the shoreline, a faint pink was all that remained of the sunset.

"I guess I better get you back to the ranch," Eric said.

"We can stay a little longer."

They stood at the lakeshore and watched the moon rise over the still water. Elsie shivered. Eric instantly removed his sports coat and put around her shoulders. She turned toward him and found his steady gaze on her face. A small thrilled of excitement shot through her stomach. He was handsome in the moonlight and very gentle with her.

"Yes, let's go back to the ranch." She looked out over the still water of the lake. It was funny, she thought, how fate sometimes brought people together.

***

They pulled into the ranch drive and Elsie directed him back to where her trailer was parked.

"Would you like to meet my horses?" she asked.

"Of course."

Elsie climbed out of the Jeep and Eric followed her, standing by the rails of the round pen in the clear moonlight. She felt her heart beat with joy at the wonderful evening and the handsome man beside her. Magic came over and sniffed first Elsie's and then Eric's hand.

Eric stood perfectly still until Magic moved on. "I'm absolutely terrified of horses," he admitted.

"Really?" Elsie said. "But you fly planes in the sky? And sometimes you crash-land?"

"I know." He paused. "It doesn't make any sense. But they seem so big and I have no idea what they're thinking."

Elsie laughed, she couldn't help it. Eric smiled and reached for her. Suddenly, she was in his arms and they both looked at each other. He bent his head and his lips touched hers. His mouth tasted like the chocolate cheesecake they had shared for dessert.

Eric pulled away and opened his eyes. "Can I see you again?" He touched her cheek with the back of his hand.

"Yes," Elsie said. She stood perfectly still with her back to the round corral as Eric got into his Jeep and pulled away. Only once the taillights disappeared, did she notice the tall shadow by the barn.

He walked toward her. She turned her back on him and climbed up the corral to perch on the top rail. He sat next to her. Magic raised his head and stared at them for a moment before going back to eating hay.

"What are you doing with a man who's scared of horses, Elsie?" Corbin spoke slowly and his tone carried none of the antagonism she had expected to hear.

"Mind your own business." She knew she should tell

him to leave before they fought.

"Look, I'm just asking. Okay?"

"You know what, he's a nice guy. He took me to dinner at a great restaurant and we never argued, not once!" She crossed her arms over her chest and wondered why she had even had one nice thought about Corbin while on her date with Eric.

"We could go to nice restaurants. But I can't promise about the arguing."

"Forget it." She climbed down from the rail and started for her trailer.

"Sorry, I was trying to be funny," Corbin said. He jumped down and landed in front of her. "Don't leave; tell me about your date."

"I'm tired and want to go to bed." She pushed against him and was again amazed at the dense coil of muscles she felt under her hands. The shape of him was solid and familiar the way a horse felt between her legs.

He grabbed her waist and pulled her against him, trapping her hands between them. She looked up to see his dark eyes. He watched her in the clear moonlight.

"Did you like it when he kissed you? I seem to remember you having more passion next to the campfire not so very long ago."

"Quit, Corbin. I thought we weren't going to talk about that."

He held her and she did not fight him; not because she couldn't get away but because some part of her loved the way his arms felt. A wrong-headed part of her, she concluded.

"You know what I think?" he said.

"I'm sure you're going to tell me."

"I think that pilot-boy isn't enough man for you. I think he's too tame for a wild, wild woman like you. What would you do with him at your ranch one day? How would he handle you training mustangs and traveling the world? He's the kind of man who wants a wife on his arm. A wife to show off at parties and make others jealous. I strongly doubt that he could stomach the real Elsie."

"This is silly. I've gone on one date with the guy," Elsie said. Her heart was beating so fast she could feel her ribs vibrating with the velocity.

He smelled like horses and wild sage and honey. She looked up again and he was waiting, bending his head to kiss her. As their lips touched, a pulse of electricity surged through her body. She untangled her arms and wrapped them around his neck, and he pulled her even closer so that their bodies were pressed together. They fit each other so well that she melded into him with the ease of a memory held in her body for too long. She let one of her hands wander down the collar of his shirt and touch the warm skin hidden underneath.

He pulled away first, and they stood together, silent. She could hear her own breathing in the still night.

"That's how a kiss should make you feel, Elsie. Anything else is just an excuse." He turned and walked back into the night.

Elsie cursed herself in every colorful manner she could remember as she undressed in the darkness of her trailer. How had she been so stupid to let Corbin know that she was still attracted to him? How dare he try to seduce her after his callous betrayal? Well, she concluded, attraction was one thing, and acting on it was another altogether. Her only goal was to train her mustang to be the best horse on competition day. She would just have to be very professional around Corbin and not let him get under her skin; she couldn't afford to let her guard down and have him thinking he had the upper hand. In fact, she couldn't afford to let her mind wander and her precious mental energy to be wasted on that man. She hung the beautiful lace dress on the doorknob. Bear Dance Ranch was a wonderful place, full of people who had welcomed her with open arms, but she couldn't let Corbin throw her into a doomed spiral. Right now, with her whole career riding on winning the contest, she needed to keep her mind clear. And how could she ever truly trust him again? He had, after all, left her when she needed him most.

CHAPTER ELEVEN

As Corbin walked away from Elsie, he let the stillness of the night calm his thundering pulse. He knew he was again in over his head with this beautiful and fiercely independent cowgirl. On the other side of the barns, he stopped and stood outside of his quarters. The moon was heavy and nearly half full. He could still feel the imprint of her body against his. He desired her, yes, but also wanted her with a longing that went soul-deep. But proving to her that he was trustworthy was harder than he had imagined. Clay was right, he would have to find a way to really apologize and explain why he had left her all those years ago. He took a deep breath, and the word *abandoned* kept floating to the surface of his mind. He ducked his head and shoved his hands deep in his pockets. He could smell the heavy, summer-laden sweetness of freshly mown alfalfa. Still, even if he didn't deserve Elsie, seeing her with that man, who could never understand her wildness, had made him all kinds of frustrated. But he knew his words of warning would only drive her further into the arms of that ridiculous pilot. He was very firmly wedged into a trap of his own making. But if that man ever hurt her, he would gladly kill him with his bare hands.

With a snort, he cut short his angry thought. Hurt her how? By convincing her to ride a crazy and wild horse? By putting her in the most dangerous situation so that he could show off in front of a crowd of people? By leaving her alone, her body broken and torn in a hospital bed? Elsie would have been better off to have never met him. All too vividly, he could remember the X-rays and the doctor discussing how to cobble her broken bones back together with metal and pins. He would never forget when they told him that she might never walk again.

He had to stop thinking. Inside his cabin, he turned on the shower and stripped down. The steam misted the mirror, nearly hiding his reflection and the dark worried eyes which stared back at him. He stepped into the shower and let the water run over his body.

His mind drifted to the morning he saw her astride her horse, nearly naked, her long thighs contoured by lean muscles. He had seen the scar, been immobilized by it. His eyes had traced the path it made as it ran the length of her femur and then skirted across her full thigh and up toward her hip. He had thought, for the thousandth time, that he was to blame for the red and purple length of it. It was, almost, as if he had branded her with his own hubris that day long ago. And so, on that morning, he'd been both frozen by her beauty—the shape of her nose and brow as she turned toward him—and also by his own guilt as he felt the depth of the way he had mishandled the woman he would always love.

He had never meant to spy upon her; he had been so overcome by the beauty and connection that she shared with her horses that day, both the wild one and the domesticated one she sat astride. There had been an effortless connection and stunning peace watching her and the animals, and he craved it even as he knew it was not for him.

The water was getting cold. Corbin stepped out of the shower. With his towel around his waist, he leaned over the sink and then looked again at his eyes in the mirror. Sure, she had kissed him back tonight, but that hardly meant all was forgiven, or even some was forgiven. He somehow doubted that he could con this girl into falling for him again—that was a scary thought. How could he get her without his charms, his bait and switch? He was so used to luring woman with a smile, a touch of the hand, and then stepping away, letting them create the allusion of the perfect man and then follow him. One thing he didn't do with women was share who he really was. Who would want a man as damaged as he?

No fun there.

He dried quickly and pulled on a loose pair of shorts and a T-shirt. He threw a few pairs of jeans and extra socks in a bag, then gathered his button-up shirts and cowboy hat. He sat down on the edge of his bed and hunted through emails on his cell phone. Briar Creek Farm in Kentucky needed help with their two-year-olds. He hadn't responded but now suddenly seemed like the perfect time. Corbin placed the call. He could breathe again with an escape route open before him.

***

Walking to the ranch house for breakfast, Elsie met Clay and they fell into stride together.

"Where's Corbin?" she said.

"He packed up and left in the middle of the night. Got a text from him this morning to say he caught a flight to Kentucky last night. Some racehorse farm needed help with their two-year-olds."

Elsie was quiet, trying to not let herself feel disappointed Corbin had not bothered to tell her this news last the night by the corral. She knew he was unreliable as hell. Why did she keep expecting him to change?

"Well, that mustang of his won't train himself," Elsie said.

"I'm sorry." Clay spoke softly.

"Don't be. I'll enjoy beating him even if he hasn't properly prepared his horse."

"I think you know what I mean." Clay held the door to the ranch house open. The smell of banana bread filled the entryway.

"I learned not to trust him a long time ago." Elsie kept her voice emotionless. "I'm a hell of a lot tougher than he is anyway."

"Believe me, I see that.

"Still, I'm sorry for how my brother acts. Some of that he learned from our Dad and some from me."

***

Three days after Corbin had suddenly left in the night, he showed back up. His pickup bounced along the drive as Elsie was bringing a group of guests down from a mountain ride. She pulled her hat down to cover her eyes and rode past the vehicle as if she hadn't even seen him sitting in the cab with his black hair messy from the wind. At the barn, as she helped guests unsaddle their horses, she heard him talking to Clay and Byron. Everyone headed in for dinner and Elsie stayed to put the last of the tack away. She heard the floorboards creak behind her and turned to find him standing in the tack room doorway.

"How was your trip?" she said. She busied her hands with hanging up a bridle.

"Good. Put the first rides on about eight young thoroughbreds," Corbin said. "So did you miss me?"

There was the joking tone to which she had grown accustomed. Suddenly, she could breathe easier; they were back on familiar ground. This was all a big joke. He would never change and she could be irritated with him.

"Oh, yeah. It was horrible: the ranch was quiet, I got ahead of you with training Magic and no one was being annoying." Her tone was light and she even rolled her eyes at him.

"Ahh, good to know I was missed," Corbin said. "So let's go up and have dinner. I hear Lenora made her famous spinach lasagna."

"Sorry, can't," Elsie said. "Eric is picking me up."

Involuntarily, she glanced up and saw a flutter of a winged shadow in his eyes, but it flew off so quickly she wondered if she had imagined it. She stood and held his eyes for a moment longer than necessary, waiting to see if this flicker might return, but it was gone. What an arrogant ass, she thought; he probably had a girlfriend or two in Kentucky. She hung a damp girth to dry and moved to the doorway. It was so much easier to be annoyed with him than to let the hurt seep in.

"Well, your loss," Corbin said.

She watched as he walked out of the barn and headed to the ranch house. Eric drove up as Corbin was only halfway to the house. She saw him stop and glance her way.

"Hey, Eric, why don't you stay for dinner?" Corbin called. "We can talk about those planes you love."

"Sure," Eric said. He got out of the Jeep and the two shook hands like old pals.

What was Corbin up to? Without a better option presenting itself, she had no choice but to walk up to where the two men stood. Eric was dressed in an expensive-looking vest and tan trousers. His dark-blond hair was closely trimmed and neat. He looked just like the kind of man Elsie should take home to show her mother and sisters that she could indeed make it in the adult world. Against her will, her eyes were drawn to Corbin and she found herself comparing the two men. Corbin was another matter—his hair was getting long, disheveled and tossed by the wind, and his jeans showed signs of working with horses all day. He had pushed his sleeves halfway up his forearms and his skin shone in the sun. When he caught her eye, the look said something so intensely intimate, she had to glance down. All she wanted to do was leave with Eric and not have to face Corbin during a whole meal.

Everyone was nice to Eric at dinner. Lenora dished up her lasagna and fresh, gluten-free rolls and of course salad and an over-sized pitcher of sangria. The evening was warm and so they ate on the back porch. The large table was bedecked with Indian Paintbrush in clay pitchers and overlooked the rolling back pasture.

Elsie was quiet, letting the conversation roll around the table as everyone ate, drank, and listened to Corbin's story about a two-year-old colt who hated the starting gate at the track. Then the conversation moved to Eric's planes and he passed around pictures of an antique twin-engine he had just purchased at auction. Elsie looked up and found Corbin watching her. She glanced down and arranged her napkin in her lap. With her temper well under control, she assured herself she could be polite and non-combative.

After dinner, Elsie and Eric walked down to the river. The breeze turned the leaves of the cottonwoods upside down and a kingfisher swooped out from a low-hanging branch.

"I like the little family you have here at the ranch. They seem like very good people," Eric said.

"They are," Elsie replied.

"I even think Corbin is warming up to me."

"Maybe." She didn't want to talk, or even think, about Corbin when she was with Eric.

Eric paused and knelt down to pick up a blue-green river stone the size of an egg. "I looked into the plight of the American Mustang after our first date.

Elsie blew out a long breath. "Bad, isn't it?"

He threw the rock into the river and stood. "I did a little searching on the Internet and what I read was astounding: the Bureau of Land Management warehouses mustangs that they round up from the wild. A lot of those horses just end up stored in holding facilities until they die, or get sick, or someone finally decides to adopt them."

"It's true." Elsie bit the inside of her cheek as she remembered the dusty and noisy holding facility where she had first laid eyes on her black mustang. "Right now, the BLM rounds up thousands of horses each year and there are already more than thirty-six thousand in holding facilities. Those horses often are never even set up to be adopted and even if they were, the average horsewomen or man could never take on the responsibility of training a wild horse. It seems hopeless, but lately, there has been some headway made with a birth control method for some mares."

The wind had picked up even more and the sinking sun turned the whole river bottom to gold. The willow along the banks was thick and the scent of Douglas fir swept down from the forests to the west. Elsie took a deep breath, and she could feel the anger and frustration at a system gone array. The only things suffering were the horses, rounded up and separated from their families and sent off to who knew where.

"The problem is that the whole system is broken and it needs to be fixed. The horses suffer, not the people. So many of the mustangs have ended up on dinner plates in Europe or Japan."

"Really?" Eric looked shocked.

"Yes. The BLM keeps getting put in a situation that's hopeless and so they tend to turn a blind eye when men with connections to Mexican meat-packing plants buy up thousands of the horses that are just waiting around to be fed taxpayer hay. It's such a huge mess."

"That's terrible." Eric took her hand and squeezed. "So when are you going to show me what you've been doing with that mustang of yours?" He stopped and faced her and raised his hand to brush a stray lock of her hair from her cheek.

"Right now?" She took Eric's hand, suddenly hopeful that he was interested in her passion for horses.

Back at the round pen, Elsie hung her brush box within easy reach. Inside the corral, she haltered Magic and led him over to sniff and investigate the equipment. He snorted and then lowered his head and cocked a hind foot, a sign he was at ease with the situation. With steady and smooth movements, Elsie groomed and picked the mustang's hooves and then led him to the middle of the pen. She then put the horse through a series of movements—asking Magic to yield his hind end, walk, trot, and canter before she finally cued him to lie down. Only once the mustang was comfortable, lying down with his legs tucked under his body, did Elsie turn to Eric.

"Wow, I can't believe you've taught him all of that," Eric said. "So you couldn't even touch him or anything before?"

"No, he was completely wild. In fact, he had been deemed unadoptable by the BLM, so if I hadn't been assigned him for the competition, then he would have gone into long-term holding or gone up for sale for one dollar," Elsie said. She rubbed Magic's neck and bent down to give him a soft kiss on his smooth, black cheek. "Tomorrow, I'll start getting him used to me sitting on his back."

"I still think you should let me put the first ride on that horse," Corbin said.

Elsie looked up from her quiet moment with her mustang to see Corbin lolling against the round pen next to Eric.

"I've been riding mine since the fourth day," Corbin said. "By the time we get to that competition, there won't be any surprises for me with my horse."

"Go away, Corbin," Elsie said. She asked Magic to stand and then gave him a small carrot piece.

"Aww, come on, El. Don't be a spoilsport and keep Eric all to yourself." Corbin's tone was antagonizing.

"Don't call me that, and seriously, GO AWAY. The last thing I need is your help with my first ride." She wanted nothing more than to scream some obscene words at Corbin but thought better of it given Eric's genteel manners.

The sound of a vehicle coming up the drive made all three of them look toward the barns and house. A white SUV with California plates stopped close to the round pen. A small blonde woman jumped out. She had a big smile on her face. "Corbin Darkhorse!" She was still beaming as she ran a hand through her hair and stretched her back.

"Katie." Corbin was smiling too. His whole face actually lit up. Elsie felt a spike of something, she hoped was not jealousy, shoot through her stomach. Corbin hugged the woman, picking her up off the ground. Eric and Elsie watched.

Corbin turned with his arm still slung over Katie's shoulders and made introductions.

"Katie is one of the editors of *Western Horsemen*," Corbin said. "The two of us have worked on a few articles over the years."

"Yes, we have." She gave him a playful push. "And I'm here to see what you're doing with this wild horse of yours. You're favored to win, of course. I keep hearing all this talk about how Corbin Darkhorse is going to be the true American Hero and save the wild horses."

"I'm not doing anything that special with my mustang, and I'm certainly not a hero. The real horse trainer is Elsie. You should see the stuff she's doing with her hers, very cutting edge." Elsie met Corbin's eyes, her face full of startled surprise. Why would he be kind to her now, she wondered. For the past month or more, he had teased her mercilessly about her slow pace.

He nodded slightly to acknowledge Elsie's shocked expression. His eyes were soft and he gave Elsie a tiny, half smile. "You know," he continued. "I think the American Mustang might need a heroine right now more than a hero, anyway."

"Really?" Katie smiled and took Elsie's hand. She seemed oblivious to the looks being passed between Elsie and Corbin.

"Could you tell me about what you're doing with your horse? And your training philosophy?" Katie said. She kept holding Elsie's hand.

Elsie glanced down, took a deep breath to calm her nerves, and then decided the woman was kind and truly interested. "Sure. Come meet Magic."

In the round pen with the mustang, Elsie worked her way through all of Magic's maneuvers. The horse was relaxed, his tail casually swishing the occasional fly. Katie took notes furiously and then ran back to her car for a camera with an expensive-looking lens.

As the sun sank low between the mountains, Elsie slipped into the world of horsemanship. She and the mustang read each minute expression, adjustment, and alignment of the other's body. She felt her breath catch in her throat when she was able to use only her fingers to direct the horse down to the ground. The dust the two stirred up filled the round pen with a soft golden haze and Elsie felt again the power of time standing still. This was the same slow magic of fate colliding with the present moment, which she had felt at the holding pens when she first met her wild horse. Carefully, her movements steady and slow, she slung her leg over the broad back of her previously wild horse. She ran her hands through his mane, letting her mind ease into the calmness of horses grazing, walking together in a herd in the moonlight, all safe, all together. She felt the horse twitch underneath her, his skin sensitive to her legs draped over his sides. He raised his head, an ear cocked back at her. She whispered softly, singing his praise while she gently urged him up to standing.

For a split second, as the mustang stood up, his

strength and power fully housed beneath her, she felt the memory of another first ride fill her whole being. Her body had stored the fear, pain, and sadness from that ill-fated day ten years ago, and now the memory came forth with such force she couldn't breathe. Her mind played the movie of the last time she rode a wild horse. She felt the terrible lurch as the mustang mare went into a hurricane of fearful bucks and lunges. Her heart began to beat with a dangerous speed. She looked at the ground and felt again the crack of her own bones, the tear as ligaments gave way, and then the swell of darkness as her head cracked into something hard. A slick sweat ran down her spine, her insides clenched with fear. She was being a fool; she chided herself for deciding to do the first fully mounted ride on Magic with an audience. Without meaning to, she glanced up and saw Katie furiously snapping pictures. Corbin stood beside her, his hands gripping the rails of the pen and his face drawn. He locked eyes with her and she saw fear mingled with pride and something akin to love but so deep it had no edge or end. She looked back down at the horse beneath her, felt his steadiness. She had prepared him for this moment, built a bond of mutual trust and respect. The horse stood steady beneath her. He was, she realized, neither worried nor inclined to throw her off. All the fear coursing through her body stemmed from her own past.

At the moment, she was perfectly safe and at peace with the powerful animal beneath her. She drew in a deep breath and exhaled. The fear drained out of her limbs, leaving her shaky but suddenly so full of hope that her whole body felt weightless. She ran one hand over the scar on her leg and the other through Magic's black mane. He turned his head and sniffed her boot, and she stroked his neck. Gently, she urged him forward. The two walked around the pen, without the constraints of leather or steel to separate them. She guided the horse with her legs and a hand on his neck. With her calves, she brushed his sides and lifted her seat into the trot. The mustang kept his inside ear latched upon Elsie and she carefully read his body and analyzed his movements—his every motion exuded trust. She took a deep breath before urging him into the canter.

Magic hesitated, both of his ears flicked back toward his rider. Very softly, almost under her breath, she said, "Canter." The mustang responded to the vocal command he had learned during their ground training sessions. He gathered his haunches underneath his body and leaped forward, carrying Elsie squarely upon his broad back. The wind rushed over her face, caressed her sides, and welcomed her; she was flying with her wild black horse. For three long strides, she closed her eyes. Silently, she gave thanks. They made two laps around the corral before Elsie slowed the horse to a walk. When she directed Magic into the middle of the arena, he responded with willingness. She slipped off his back and then wrapped her arms around his neck. For a few long moments, she stood still, her face buried in his velvet coat as she choked back the tears of pure gratitude that stung her eyes.

Her legs were shaking and a giddy joy filled her heart: she had ridden her mustang!

When she finally stepped away from the animal, the small group gathered at the round pen clapped. She saw that Eric was grinning at her and Katie's cheeks were flushed as she looked through the images on her camera's viewfinder. Corbin was completely still, his hands still holding the top rail.

"That was amazing!" Katie exclaimed. "I've never seen anything like it before. And the images are so cool! The dust and with the sun filtering through lends them an otherworldly feel."

"Good job, Elsie," Eric said.

Corbin was silent and only once Elsie stood outside the pen did she meet his eyes and see something so tender and worried and soft that she felt her heartbeat pick up speed again. Suddenly, she wished that they were alone, that she could've shared this moment with just Corbin. She knew the past, filled with a trauma they had experienced together, was being both healed and eased with her ride on the Magic. But they weren't alone and Eric pulled her against him and kissed her swiftly on the lips. She stood still and closed her eyes, and when she opened them, Corbin was gone.

"Can you tell me about your accident?" Katie said. "I hope you don't mind me asking, but I think it's part of your story. I think you might just be the next Mustang Annie."

"Of course," Elsie said. She took a breath and began at the beginning.

***

Corbin walked away. His palms were sweaty. He wanted to hit something, preferably Eric's smug face. He had barely been able to watch Elsie as she mounted and then rode her mustang without any tack. For the first couple of minutes into her ride, he had wanted to open the round pen gate, walk in, and snatch her off the horse. Of course, that would have only made her spitting-mad but at least he would have been able to breathe. As he watched her sitting on the black horse, his mind was filled with the memories and smells of that fateful day. He could still taste his own fear, coppery like blood, and feel the surge of adrenaline as he pulled her from under the hooves of the mustang mare. She had been limp at that point, and for two long and terrible minutes, he had held her and been convinced she was lifeless. When her breath came shuddering back, he had brushed his lips along her bloody forehead and thanked God with more sincerity than he had ever had the need to do before. Her leg had been twisted and mangled and the femur bone poked through her jeans. The arena smelled of fear—that of the horse and

Corbin. He would never forget how it had stuck in his nostrils for days, like dried sweat and rust.

He had never been in love before, never knew what it was like to feel so helpless as he saw the girl, who he thought was stronger than anyone in the whole world, lying limp in his lap. Two months earlier, he had first laid eyes on her. She was sitting on her chestnut gelding and he had barely been able to breathe. She was wearing dirty jeans and a T-shirt, her hair was loose down her back and wavy like she had just been to the beach. As he stared, she turned and looked at him, her eyes alive with so much life he found himself unable to look away. It was, even now in his memory, like she glowed from within. Almost as if her skin was thin enough that a bit of her beautiful soul shone through. He watched in admiration as she put her young horse through a series of cantering exercises until the animal was supple and smooth under her seat, and then she began showing the gelding how to change his canter leads. She was careful and steady and when the horse become a little nervous, she brought him back down to a trot. Her trainer walked over and the two of them talked and she tried again. As the chestnut leaped into the correct lead, the look of sheer joy on her face made Corbin's breath catch again in his throat.

He waited until she was finished and then followed her out of the schooling arena. In the dusk of evening, horses and grooms milling around the busy show grounds, he caught up to her and offered his hand. "I'm Corbin Darkhorse."

She had looked at him, her eyebrows drawn together before she took his hand. She said simply, "Elsie."

"Can I buy you dinner?" He had exactly $22.11 in his pocket and he had hoped to make it last until tomorrow night where he planned to win the jackpot at the competition. At nineteen years old, he was living the dream of many young horse trainers on the show circuit, but he was also very broke.

"I have twenty horses to feed and groom tonight," she said in way of an answer.

"I'll help," he replied, even though he too had training horses to care for and tack to clean for the show tomorrow. He knew at that moment he would stay up all night and do all her chores if she would

just have one meal with him.

She seemed to be weighing his offer as they walked back toward the rows of stalls. The sounds of horses calling to each other and the chatter from clusters of clients heading off to dinner dropped away, Corbin watched her face as they made their way through the melee of the backgrounds of a horse show. She had serious eyes with a generous mouth that tipped up in the corners, lending her face a quiet softness.

She stopped and faced him; her dark, arching brows drew together once more. He noticed that she had a smudge of dust running from her cheekbone to her left ear. He resisted the urge to brush it away with his thumb.

"Okay. You can take me to dinner."

He grinned and took the grooming box she offered. After she had untacked her chestnut gelding and bathed him, she came and helped Corbin move down the line of show horses. With the steady movement of a brush running over glistening equine hides, they began to learn about each other. By the time they had fed the horses and then moved off to care for Corbin's small string of reining colts, he knew that she was fiercely independent, didn't want to be a nurse like the other females in her family, and was head-over-heels in love with everything equine.

Finally, both dirty and exhausted, they ordered tacos at a tiny all-night diner. Corbin was so in love with her by that point, that when she licked salsa from her fingers and flashed him a fast and shy smile, he couldn't think clearly.

He had walked her back to the stalls where her trainer had the horses stabled.

"Can I take you on a proper date tomorrow after I win the derby jackpot?" he asked.

"You know you'll win?" She looked doubtful.

Emboldened, he took her hand. A jolt of electricity moved up his arm and her fingers twitched in his grasp. She looked up at him. Surprise and incredulous wonder showed on her face. He bent down and kissed her lips before she could speak, or he lost the nerve to be so bold. For a moment, she tensed against him before slowly melting forward until he held her in his arms. She was both lean and strong and yet her lips were very soft and full. When he breathed her in, he smelled sweat and horses, and then something so sweet that it reminded him of the wild honeysuckle growing on the fence next to his childhood home. At that moment, he was completely hers without even knowing what that really meant.

She pulled back and he could barely breathe. He knew a silly smile was plastered on his face. Her nostrils were flared and her eyes searched his. He cupped her cheek in his palm and brushed his thumb along the smudge of dirt. They could have been alone on a mountaintop, the world stretching away below them, instead of a gravel parking lot next to rows of stalls and tired horses eating hay. Grooms and riders were still getting ready for the next day and an occasional whinny cut through the night air as horses were led back to the stalls, their coats slick with sweat.

Corbin wished they were alone. This was the kind of girl he could take riding in the high country at the north end of the reservation. He could just tell she would appreciate the shadows as the sun sank low and the eager canter of his mother's homebred mares. But he was getting away with the future. He still had to convince her to go on another date with him the following evening.

"I know," he whispered, surprised that his voice was as weak as his legs. "Because I can feel it."

"You can?" She tilted her head and looked at him.

Suddenly, he wasn't sure if she was referring to the horse show or the kiss they had just shared. Her brown eyes were huge in the moonlight and there were dark shadows under them. He knew he needed to let her get some rest but he didn't want to release her from his arms.

He decided to stick with the spoken and leave some magic silent between them. "When I win tomorrow night, I'll have enough money to get both of us set up with a nice little barn for a couple of months. We could get that horse of yours going really well and then we could enter some of those colt-starting competitions for some fast cash on the side. We could make a go of it, you and me, Elsie. I know we can." The words spilled out fast. He hadn't realized he was going to ask her to come with him until he spoke. But it was true, he wanted her to come. He had barely known Elsie for six hours and yet he could not imagine his life without her.

She pulled away, her eyes fearful and suddenly guarded. "We don't even know each other."

He knew now was the time to say something romantic, something that would let her know he was trustworthy. Nothing came to his mind and so he looked at the dirt and kicked a rock around with the toe of his boot. She was slipping away. The sound of a diesel truck starting behind them, and then the flood of light as the driver flicked on their headlights and pulled away, wedged between them. She had stepped farther away from him, and her face was distrustful. He took a deep breath and knew it was now or never. "I know this sounds crazy, but this is the best night of my life and I want to have twenty-five thousand more." How true his words were. He was not sure he had ever felt more alive than when he stood next to her.

She stopped backing away; he stepped forward to close the gap between them. "Just think about it, okay, please?"

"I will," she said before turning into the darkness and walking away from him.

Corbin didn't see her at all the next day. He was busy warming up his horses and then preparing for the derby that night. Each time he went by the stalls, where the horses she cared for were stabled, she was either out warming up a young horse or organizing the horse owners for their classes. Had she woken up that morning and thought about him? He stood still, his hand resting on the neck of his horse, hoping she had. At the end of the day, after all the amateur riders had already shown their horses, the big tractor came in and groomed the arena for the professional derby. Corbin's stomach was all butterflies as he oiled his saddle and then wrapped Nighthawk's legs with neat white polos.

Inside the arena, the judges were seated ahead of him and the lights so bright he had to blink. He said a silent and fast prayer and then urged his horse into a canter. Time slowed down and he felt the position of his leg on Nighthawk's side, the depth of his seat in the saddle, and the surge of adrenaline that always waited for him in the show ring. He shifted to the left before the side-pass and then felt the gelding move to follow his weight. The flying changes-of-lead were smooth and easy and he grinned, enjoying the way the horse responded to his most subtle of cues. It felt as if they were at home practicing in the big fields. When he finally set his hand down on the horse's withers and looked up, the crowd was clapping and whistles cut through the air. He searched the faces in the crowd, looking for a girl with large brown eyes. Finally, he spotted her; his whole face broke out in a smile as he realized she was waving to him, her long hair glowing in the overhead lights.

At that moment, he had thought his whole life was set—the girl he would marry, the career as a horse trainer—all unfolding before him with both ease and beauty. Only later would he look back on that moment and realize what hubris it had been to think that he was owed this natural progression of happiness.

CHAPTER TWELVE

Alone in her small bed, the adrenaline long since drained from her body, Elsie fell into the space between waking and sleeping.

"You left!" Her voice rose. "You left me!" All her well-controlled rage burst the dam of her resolve and tumbled forward angry and truthful. She turned away, unable to look at him. Blood coursed so quickly through her veins it was hard to breathe. When she turned back to him, his whole body softened toward her.

"I know." He reached his hands out. His eyes were clear and so sad she took a step back. "I've hated myself for a long time because of what I did that day."

"Why?" Her anger was high and tight in her chest. She knew what he said next would turn her insides to liquid fire and forever burn the connection they had once shared. Or perhaps, she would finally know what Corbin had really felt all those years ago and somehow rectify her memories of the past with the man she was getting to know all over again.

"Fear." He met her questioning gaze with an unflinching stare. "And shame. I had gotten you into that wreck. I was scared. It seemed easier to leave." He still met her eyes. "Now, today, I realize how wrong I was. The more I ran, the worse I felt. But I ran for a

long time, Elsie. I ran until I had nowhere else to go and then I turned around and faced up to my fears. I've known for a long time that Clay wasn't like our dad, but I wasn't so sure about myself."

He finally glanced down, shifting his weight for a moment and then looked back up. His eyes were those of a man who had faced his own demons. "I realized I could be the man I wanted to be—father be damned. And that's what I've done ever since. I've been me. But I'm sorrier than I can say or than I can show you for what I did to you. I've never loved anyone the way I love you, Elsie. I was a boy when I felt it the first time and it shook me pretty good. But now I'm a man and though it still shakes me, I'm all yours. Every inch of me wants to know that maybe you could one day love me just a tenth of the amount that I love you."

Elsie was silent. She had no idea what to say. Her heart had kicked up to a speed that made it hard to think at all and she was having trouble breathing.

"Elsie?" He stepped closer to her.

Now, she could barely draw a breath. She wanted to say something, anything. Where were her angry words, her smart comebacks?

"Can I hold you?"

She nodded.

"Damn it." He spoke as he grabbed her, pulling her against him. He wrapped her in his arms, pushed her face into his neck and then held the back of her head, as gentle as if she were a newborn child. "I love you," he whispered into her hair and then kissed along her temple and pulled her even closer to his body. She felt her insides unclench. He held her firmly against him and she felt her breathing slow and calm and her stomach relax. Her heartbeat steadied and she let her nostrils breathe in the scent of wild sage and mountains and alfalfa hay which clung to his skin. Her nose rested in the hollow at the base of his neck where his breastbone crested. His skin was soft and a tiny bit salty, and she felt herself slowly bring her lips together and touch his warm skin. With the brush of her mouth, he pulled her closer still and she lifted her arms and wrapped them around his neck. "I'm so sorry," he whispered again into her hair as he smoothed and touched until she melted into his body.

The dream was so vivid that Elsie woke with Corbin's name on her lips. Her whole body was damp with sweat and the bedsheets were twisted around her legs. She lay still and listened to the opening trill of birdsong as morning overtook the ranch. Riding Magic for the first time the night before had brought back so many memories from the accident. For a long, long time after the wild horse had broken her body, she had dreamed of Corbin Darkhorse each night. The dreams were filled with a sad mix of their short time together and a pain so intense she had often woken with her hand clutching at her stomach. Very slowly, as her body healed and she learned to walk again, she had trained her mind with anger and steeled herself to keep him from her dreams. But now he filled up her waking life again and somehow was slipping back into her nights as well.

"Leave me alone," she said out loud and then got out of bed. All she wanted was for Corbin to stay away from her. She had, after all, ridden her wild horse the previous night and somehow the magic that was between them had been caught on camera. Her career, which had been derailed for so long, was beginning to come together again with the aid of this mustang. But how strange that just as she made her comeback, Corbin also entered her life and filled her with fear. She couldn't afford to be caught and pulled away in the mad swirl of intoxication that was Corbin Darkhorse. When she had met him all those years ago, she had thought that, finally, here was a man who could keep up with her dreams, of horses, adventure, and creating a career as big and bright as the western sky. But he had proven that he was as fickle and unreliable as spring sunshine.

She dressed quickly and then stepped out into the morning mist; she would not waste any more of her precious energy thinking about Corbin or the past. Ahead of her was once again a chance to have the career of her dreams.

Magic waited for her, his eyes deep pools of darkness as the first rays of the sun caught in his black mane. She kissed his velvet nose and whispered a few sweet-nothings. She would never let another horse trainer catch her telling her mustang how much she loved his black coat, or the way the wind ruffled his mane, but when they were alone, she could simply be a girl with her horse and so happy her heart might burst from her chest and go sing with the red-winged black birds in the cattails. "Last night was pure bliss. Last night you let me dance with you." The horse looked at her and lipped her hair. His eyes were soft and trusting. They had so much more work to do before the competition, she knew this, but right now she wanted to bask in their accomplishment.

As Elsie walked toward the house to gather the group of guests she would pair with appropriate mounts for the week, she saw Eric's Jeep coming up the gravel drive. She waited for him to stop and jump out of the vehicle. A gust of wind blew her hair in her eyes and when she brushed it away, he was standing in front of her with a long-stemmed red rose.

"For yesterday," he said.

She felt her cheeks heating up. This sexy man was taking his time and really trying to win her. How good it felt to actually be treated so gently. "Thank you."

"I was so impressed by how you rode that wild horse. It was like watching a movie." He pulled Elsie to him and wrapped his arms around her. "Can I steal you away for the weekend?"

Her heart began to beat faster. Just the two of them alone—suddenly, it seemed riskier than riding her wild horse. She swallowed down her unease and smiled up at Eric.

"To Denver, or San Francisco? We could go wherever you want? Escape the mountains for a bit and eat at a decent restaurant for a change."

"I'd love to go away with you. I better make sure Lenora and Clay can spare me." She stepped out of his arms and smoothed her hair back from her face. "Just surprise me on the location."

"Deal." He grabbed her waist again and pulled her close to him. She looked up and felt her heart flutter when she looked into his eyes. She ran her fingertips across the stubble of his chin and along the strong line of his jaw. When he bent his head, she closed her eyes. His lips were cool and soft on hers. A tingle ran up her spine and along her ribs, making her sigh with relief. There was attraction, maybe even passion lurking in Eric, she just knew it. Not every kiss had to be so scorching hot that it left her weak and vulnerable. Maybe it would even be nice to be able to think coherently when she was around her date.

"I better get back to work," Elsie said.

"Of course." He stepped away but held her hand for a moment longer. "I'll pick you up Friday night. We'll take my plane."

All morning on the ride along the stream, a line of guests on horses behind her, Elsie tried to put Corbin out of her mind. Riding Magic last night, sitting on his broad back and feeling the panic fill her whole body as she knew that once again she was at the mercy of a large and mostly wild horse, had left her a little raw. Corbin had witnessed both of her mustang rides. He had been the one to pull her from the terrified and destructive mare all those years ago and he had also been the man to leave her broken, not only physically but emotionally, in a hospital bed. Her dream had been so vivid and she could still taste the salt from his skin on her lips as if the kiss had been real. Going away with Eric would be the best way to end her stirred-up feelings for Corbin.

***

He rested against the corral panels and waited for her.

Corbin knew Lenora had lent Elsie a dress again. A deadly calm had fallen over his mind. He left her in a hospital bed all those years ago and now she was moving into the arms of another man. Eric was a decent enough human, Corbin thought, if he was honest with himself, but Elsie belonged with him. He rocked back on his boot heels. He had no one to blame for the current situation but himself. Yet, all anger and frustration aside, he knew that Eric didn't understand Elsie. Her passion and fire would confuse that man. Corbin looked down at the ground, realizing that he was only now truly appreciating Elsie's wild spirit. Most of the time he was too angry with her to realize that she was simply being herself: a passionate woman who couldn't hold back with anything in life. He knew that was one of the qualities which had drawn him to her in the beginning. Only lately, with guilt and shame heavy on his shoulders, had his previous admiration for her independent ways turned to anger and frustration. He knew, instinctually, that the very things which now made her so hard to win back were the traits he so admired and also desired in an equal, a partner and a lover.

He heard her coming; the slight drag of her boot heel from the injured leg, giving her away her identity. He closed his eyes for a moment as the guilt washed through his heart. He took a deep breath; he had no more time to back down when faced with his own disgraceful behavior in the past.

"If it doesn't work out, Elsie. Just call me and I'll come and get you."

He didn't turn even as he knew she had climbed the two steps to her trailer. He heard the door open and then she spoke. "Thank you."

He walked away without seeing what dress she wore. It would be better this way, he thought, less painful if she chose Eric.

He walked into the rays of setting sun, trying not to feel sorry for himself. Angry, yes, he could feel angry. Part of him wanted to drive into town and have a drink at the Painted Pony. Well, more than a drink. He wanted to forget both the past and the present. He reached for his phone and started searching through contacts. He would go to Kentucky or New York or Texas. Somewhere they would welcome him, praise him for being the horse trainer who didn't want to be tied down, who roamed and wandered. There were plenty of horse-crazy women in this world and he had the words to make them all think he was their very own native cowboy. He stopped and looked at the plume of dust kicked up by Eric's Jeep as it pulled up to the ranch. He waited for the pilot to climb out.

"Evening," he said.

Eric smiled and closed the door of his Jeep. "Great weather, isn't it? I love this country in the summer."

"Be good to her." Corbin had no desire to make small talk with this man and so he turned and walked away. He knew he couldn't run this time. If she needed him, he had to be ready. There was no other option or choice. He stood for a moment and looked at his truck. He could leave; it would be so easy, almost like slipping into a pre-worn pair of jeans, already molded by previous use.

Instead, he went to saddle his mustang. Even if he lost her forever, he had to at least try. He had to be there for her if she ever needed him again.

CHRISTINA RHOADS

CHAPTER THIRTEEN

Elsie heard the Jeep pull up. She grabbed her overnight bag, adjusted her dress, and took a deep breath to steady her nerves. They were just going away for the weekend, she reminded herself.

Outside, in the golden light of evening, she turned and blew a quick kiss to her horses nibbling on grass in their corral. Eric strode toward her and she smiled. He wore pressed pants and a white shirt and looked very much the part of the handsome pilot.

"Ready for a little adventure?" he asked as he took her bag.

"I was born ready." She felt her spirits lift. She had just felt a little touch of nerves before, she assured herself.

On the landing strip in Kalispell, a small jet waited for them. "It's not an antique," Eric said. He was smiling and she could see how happy he was to be sharing his love of flying. "This is a Citation and the first jet I learned to fly."

Eric spoke to the attendant and then helped her into her seat in the cockpit. He buckled her in, adjusted her headset, and then kissed her on the lips before climbing into his seat. The sun was just starting to dip below the

155

lake as he powered up the plane and went through a series of checks. He was matter-of-fact as he explained what he was doing. It was only as the plane lifted from the runway, and the mountains and Flathead Lake fell away below them, that Elsie's stomach tightened in apprehension. She turned to look at Eric sitting next to her. His face was calm and his brow furrowed slightly in concentration. This was what she wanted, a man who was nothing like Corbin Darkhorse.

Eric had a car waiting for them in Denver. The city was alive and Elsie felt her pulse racing as they drove through the brightly lit streets. She had been living in the mountains, on a very secluded ranch all summer, and the buzz of cars and people set her nerves on edge. They stopped next to the Brown Palace and Eric helped her with her bag. As they rode the elevator up to the fifth floor, Elsie realized they hadn't talked about the sleeping arrangements. She glanced down at the silky folds of her dress and felt her face flush. If this were Corbin, she would simply demand her own bed and space, but Eric had been so kind and gentle with her. Somehow, she felt as if she owed him something. She looked up and found him watching her. He stepped close and took her hand. In the mirrored wall, she saw her eyes, large and scared. She swallowed, her whole body suddenly going cold.

"You look stunning tonight," he said. "I can't imagine how beautiful you will be after a manicure and a facial. I think tomorrow we take advantage of the spa." Eric ran his thumb along her jawline. He bent his head and she closed her eyes as his lips touched her own. A wave of panic swept through her whole body, and she clenched her hand on her bag. In her mind, she saw Corbin standing next to the round pen where her horses ate hay. He had seemed so sincere as he spoke before she left for her trip with Eric. When her anger deserted her, she was suddenly able to see him as he the nineteen-year-old boy/man, his dark eyes eager as he talked about their future together. Eric's lips were on her neck and all she could think about was Corbin Darkhorse. She knew she had to calm her mind, concentrate on the moment. Corbin had proven his unreliability years before. Eric seemed both stable and solid. She pushed down her growing unease and slipped her free arm around the pilot's neck.

"Let's order room service," he whispered in her ear. "I'm dying to see what's under that dress."

A sick knot settled in the bottom of her ribcage. The door to the elevator pinged open and Eric led the way to their room. The thick carpet muffled their steps and when Eric stopped at the door, he smiled at her before inserting the key. A buzzing began to fill Elsie's ears and she took a couple of quick breaths. For a moment, she worried that she would be sick to her stomach or pass out. She tried to tell herself it was just jitters. Eric was an attractive man with a lot to offer. She would be able to travel and see some of the world and afford her horses, she told herself. Unbidden, his flippant statement to Corbin came back to her mind. How could he assume she would give up training horses just because they got married? She smiled as best she could and excused herself to the bathroom without even enjoying the elegant but understated furniture and heavy curtains opening to a view of the city stretching below.

Inside the bathroom, she stared at her perfectly made-up face in the mirror. She attempted to calm her mind by taking three deep breaths. What was her churning stomach and buzzing head telling her? She stilled her mind and listened. With her anger and hurt layered about her, she had forgotten who she was. She had, once again, not listened to her gut. The last time she had made that mistake, she had ended up nearly trampled to death by a wild horse, now she was about to commit to a man who was wrong for her. She closed her eyes and saw Corbin looking at her, the night sky above him and his eyes soft and playful.

Leave. She felt the word and the urgency rush through her as if brought on a gust of westerly wind. She took a couple of deep breaths and then walked out of the bathroom to find Eric pouring champagne; he took her in his arms and began to kiss a trail down her neck. Frozen, she felt her skin go cold and her stomach knotted even further—she knew this was wrong. She tried to close her eyes but again she saw Corbin. This time he was holding his hand out, helping her up behind him on Nighthawk. She felt his electric strength under her hands as she held onto him and the horse beneath them surged forward. She opened her eyes and stepped away from Eric. Seeming confused, he grabbed her shoulders.

"What's wrong?" He sounded hurt.

Elsie kept backing away from him, and with each step, the sick feeling below her ribs eased. She edged toward the door. "I'm sorry, I can't do this."

"What? Elsie, stop. Where are you going?"

"I'm so sorry," she said again. She grabbed her overnight bag from the armchair.

"This is ridiculous, we've been going out for a month or more," he said. "I've been so patient with you and never pushed."

Elsie grabbed the door handle and was about to open the door when he put his hand up to stop her.

"Elsie, look at me! What is wrong?" His face was turning red and she felt her instincts telling her to leave, quickly. If he were a horse, she knew that he was about to do something unpredictable and maybe dangerous.

"What did I do wrong?" Eric said. "I've been attentive to your horse stories and tried to show you a good time, and this is how you repay me?"

Elsie stood up as tall as her five-foot, four-inch frame would allow her, threw her shoulders back, and took a deep breath. "Eric, you're a great guy but I have to go. RIGHT NOW!"

He still stood in her way. His blue eyes had gone cold and his lips were pale at the corners.

"Eric, please move," she said.

"It's that cowboy, isn't it? The Indian one?" His voice was very low.

"No," she said. "We aren't right for each other. I don't know if Corbin is right for me either, but, somehow, that's beside the point right now." She held his eyes and he finally looked down and stepped out of her way. She pulled the door open and was out in the hall, her heart pounding, in less than a second.

"I'm a hell of a catch. He's just some poor horse trainer. He could never give you what I can," Eric called behind her.

She didn't look back. From a logical standpoint, Eric was right, he was the better choice. Yet this moment in time had nothing to do with logic and everything to do with her whole body, heart, and soul telling her she could not be with a man just because he was the *right choice*. She knew true love. Yes, it was a long time ago, and she had no idea if she would ever feel it again, but it seemed less than honest to pretend with a man she knew she could never love with the same depth of spirit and soul with which she had connected to Corbin Darkhorse. She'd been young, but she had experienced passion so intense it had nearly burned away her whole existence, and she could never settle for less. Even if Eric bought her a barn full of horses, and a ranch all of her own, she could not love him the way she had once loved Corbin.

She charged past the elevator. The idea of being caught behind the gilded doors made her head for the stairs. She should have never gotten off that thing, she realized, once she saw her scared face in the mirrored sides. She shoved open the door and limped her way down the stairs in the less-than-sensible shoes which Lenora had lent her. The night air was cool on her face as she pushed her way out of the fancy hotel and out onto the street. The doorman followed her out. "Miss? Are you okay?"

She realized her hair was a wild tangle and her eyes must still be huge. "Yes, I'm fine." Her words sounded too high-pitched to her ears and so she took a deep breath and smiled as best she could.

"Do you need a taxi?" The doorman was already waving down a yellow cab as it passed.

"Thank you." Once inside, she fumbled in her purse, looking for a tip for the kind man.

"No," he said, waving his hand. "Safe travels, Miss. May you find what you're looking for."

At the airport, she charged a plane ticket to her credit card. While the attendant ran the card, she kept her fingers crossed behind her back, praying it would not be declined. At her boarding gate, she called her mother. No answer. She called Bear Dance Ranch. It was late and she knew the chances of someone still being up were slim. Nothing. Finally, she called his number.

"Hello." His voice was low as if he had been asleep.

Warmth, relief, and a deep sense of safety flooded through her body. She felt dizzy and closed her eyes, leaning back in her seat.

"Could you come pick me up at the airport?" She spoke carefully as tears pricked her eyelids.

"Of course. Are you okay?"

"Yes, I just need to come home." She kept her voice steady to the very end.

It was nearly morning, the sky a pale-pink like the inside of a columbine flower, when Elsie stepped out of the baggage claim and saw Corbin's truck idling next to the sidewalk. He got out and grabbed her bag and then pulled her into his arms for a hug. She felt the first tears burning her throat and tried to swallow them down as she blinked. He stepped back and studied her face; his brows were drawn together with worry and his eyes gentle.

"You're all right now. I have you," he said and then pulled her back into his arms.

She didn't resist him. "I still haven't forgiven you," she whispered against his neck, even as she breathed in the smell of pines forests, saddle soap, and sage.

"I know." He bent his head so that their cheeks brushed together. "I'm just glad you're coming back to the ranch."

Elsie was the first to back away. He let her go, shifting his hands into his pockets. She didn't look up until nearly a meter separated them. When she did meet his eyes, she saw that he looked tired; his cheeks dark with stubble and eyes heavy-lidded. She wanted to say something smart and maybe a little sharp. She felt around, trying to grasp the old anger, but it was conspicuously absent.

"Come on, let's get you home." He opened the passenger side door for her and she climbed in, silent. Without her anger, without the past between them, she didn't know what to say to Corbin. She thought she knew everything about this man and suddenly, she realized, what she did know was so limited to the past and maybe even obsolete.

They were silent as they drove into the early-morning sunrise. Elsie's phone started to ring and she ignored it.

"I'd say that I'd talk to him for you, but I know you, Elsie. You can handle him better than I ever could."

"Thanks," she said. "I think I said everything to him already."

"You're not hurt in any way? Right?" He looked away from the road for far longer than he should have, searching her face with his dark gaze.

"No, not at all. I guess I just finally realized that he wasn't that into the real me, he only liked the idea of the girl who trained wild horses," Elsie replied.

Corbin was silent as the road wound up. The mountains opened their arms and welcomed her home.

When he did speak, his voice was low, persuasive, as if

she were a skittish horse. "I'm going home tomorrow for dinner with my mother. Would you come with me?" He paused. "It's not the Brown Palace in Denver, but my mom can cook."

He shot her a quick flash of a smile, one she had not seen before. Was he shy?

Elsie felt her heart jump. This was altogether different from the sick feeling she had felt below her ribs only a few hours earlier. "Yes, I'd like that," she replied.

CHAPTER FOURTEEN

Early the following morning, Elsie and Corbin loaded the mustangs in the horse trailer. "Wait." He spoke as he stepped to the passenger side of the truck. "Let me get the door."

"I thought I was driving?" she said with a very straight face.

"Okay. You drive. But I'm opening that door for you as well."

She laughed. "You can drive."

"A test, huh?" He held the passenger door open for her and she slipped inside. He smelled like the forests of lodgepole pine. Inside the truck, she found a buddle of freshly picked mountain asters. They still had dewdrops clinging to their lavender petals.

"Thank you." She looked at him as he climbed into the driver's seat.

"You're welcome." He flashed her that shy smile again and started the engine.

The mist was rising from the river and the sun cast the whole valley in gold as they drove down the dusty road away from the ranch. Sandbar willow and alder lined the riverbank, their leaves still damp from the night. Lenora had packed them a basket for the trip and Elsie opened it to find fresh-baked banana-nut bread, strawberries, salty cheese, and hard-boiled eggs. It was good to feel loved. They listened to an old Merle Haggard song and Elsie closed her eyes and felt the early-fall breeze on her face. When she opened them, Corbin was looking at her, but he quickly returned his gaze to the road ahead. Her stomach did that quick flip again. She sat up in the bench seat of the old truck and reached out to touch the black hair around his ear. He was getting shaggy. He caught her hand in his and brought it his lips so quickly, her breath stuck in her throat. They were on a straight stretch of road and he turned, his eyes intense. Elsie couldn't look away. Shivers ran up the outsides of her thighs, across her rib cage, and whispered below the swell of her breasts. The road curved and he released her hand as his eyes went back to the road. She could breathe again. Her hand trembling just a little, she searched for a new radio station. She wondered briefly at how much her heart had changed since leaving Eric at the hotel in Denver. Yet she wasn't sure she could trust this new feeling or Corbin.

The reservation was just like nearly every other poor part of Montana, only worse: a few cars on blocks, houses not always finished, prairie taking over the fields and yards. On the east side of the continental divide, the land was more rolling and the pines twisted by the constant wind. Elsie sat up and tried to see a young Corbin following his brother around. What had his upbringing taught him, shown him that her own had not? They pulled down a long dirt road, wound up and sideways, until she saw the barn come into view and a few paint horses. When they stopped the truck and Elsie shoved out of the truck door, she was met by the damp, black noses of a few dogs with fast-wagging tails. She touched their heads and pushed their impolite noses away from her before stroking their long ears. When she looked up, a tall woman with sharp eyes stood next to the truck.

"Mom, this is Elsie," Corbin said. "Elsie, my mother, Raina Darkhorse."

"Hi," Elsie said. She took Raina's hand and tried her best not to flinch away from the woman's clear eyes, so much like Corbin's but even darker.

Finally, she smiled, showing even white teeth as perfect as her son's. "Welcome, Elsie," Raina said. "You should know that Corbin has never, ever, brought a girl home before. He must think you have the mettle to handle me."

Elsie felt her smile stiffen on her lips and she swallowed, then Raina winked and Corbin laughed. Elsie felt herself blush and then grinned back at Raina who she found herself liking. They unloaded the horses and put them in a small corral off the barn, and then went in for a lunch of cornbread and black beans. Corbin told Raina the news from Bear Dance Ranch and Elsie enjoyed stealing glances around the small cabin. A woodstove sat in one corner and a row of windows opened to the east and west sides of the house, utilizing the natural light from both sunrise and sunset. In the far corner, an easel stood with a half-finished painting of the hills and a strange-looking, golden sky.

After lunch, they tacked up the horses. Corbin was flirting in a gentle way—he held her bridle for her, offered her a leg-up in the saddle. Then he rested his hand on her thigh, looking at her. The sun was in his eyes. He blinked, his face still of expression yet his eyes so alive.

"You sit a horse better than anyone I know, El," he said. Corbin ran his hand down to her knee cap and he looked off to the east, then back at her. His eyes were open and clear. Her heart lurched so violently she nearly choked, and her pulse quickened. It was shocking how her whole body reacted to this man with such speedy need.

His fingers felt back up her leg, following the fault line of her scar. "I'm sorry I wasn't there when you needed me most."

"I know you are." Her voice was low. As she spoke, she felt her heart soften a little, the way it did when Magic turned to look at her early in the mornings, or when she felt the tickle of equine whiskers on her open palm.

"Would you go to dinner with me at Wolf's Peak tomorrow night? I promise I'll be a perfect gentleman."

Elsie felt her mouth go dry. She could see her pulse jumping wildly on the hand holding the reins and she quickly pulled her sleeve down. The last thing she wanted was for Corbin to know that she wanted him, a lot. In fact, part of her didn't want him to be a gentleman. She secretly realized she wanted him to dare her, like the night in the mountains, she wanted to feel him touch and stroke her and bring her deeply hidden fire to the surface. She looked away from his searching eyes and tried to calm her heart. It was hard to swallow so she could speak.

"I'd like that, Corbin," she said.

He grinned, his face boyish with his enthusiasm. His eyes were full of laughter and he winked as he leaped onto his horse. "Race you to the high gap?" He pointed up into the pasture where the hill crested and a trail led toward the granite peaks.

"You're on. Let's see how well broke these mustangs really are." Elise set her hand in Magic's mane and urged him forward with her calves. The horse responded, gathering his haunches and springing forward, neck-to-neck with Corbin's gray mount. They raced up through the pasture, the ground rising rapidly under their horses' hooves until they slowed at the top of the rise. They paused, their horses blowing and stamping, excited by the fast gallop and eager for more even as they regained their wind in the thin mountain air. The cabin where Corbin had grown up was far below them. Elsie turned and found him watching her. His face was still and his eyes dark and quiet. He had changed over the last ten years. Of course, she could still see the impatient and eager teenager, holding her hand even as he spoke in rapids bursts about his dreams and the trophies he would win. Yet, as she looked closer, a different man sat on his horse next to her. He was still fiery and often too eager, but he seemed softer around the edges and she realized she might like the person he was becoming. Elsie smoothed Magic's black mane to the side and took a deep breath. Just two days ago, she had planned to never willingly spend any time alone with Corbin Darkhorse and now she found herself admiring his change in character. She knew she needed to think this all through. The rush of emotion and her body's adverse reaction to Eric had surprised her. She had known that she was still attracted to Corbin, but she had chalked that up to a silly remembrance of her first love and a hot summer romance. Now, in the light of day, the wind teasing her hair free of its braid, she felt the reality of her change of heart. For so long, she had fought what her heart was telling her. She just wasn't sure she was ready to tell Corbin how complete this change really was. Avoiding his eyes, she urged her mustang onward.

They rode up into the hills. Tall grass brushed against their boots and the horses' bellies. Wild sage grew next to large boulders and the sun warmed their shoulders. They seldom spoke and Elsie let her mind relax into the flow of movement of the horse beneath her. Magic responded beautifully to her aids as she directed him through the rugged terrain.

At the top of the westernmost hill, they discovered a stretch of downed fence. Corbin dismounted and pulled out his fencing pliers. Elsie tied the horses off to a post and helped him re-stretch the wire. Higher to the north, where the grass ended and the tree line rimmed the mountains in heavy green furs, a tiny cabin nestled.

"Is it abandoned?" Elsie asked. She jerked her chin in the direction of the mountains and cabin.

"Sort of. Want to ride over and check it out?" His eyes were steady as he spoke and so gentle that Elsie forgot, for a moment, to whom she was speaking. This man was changing while she watched. Yet she knew this wasn't true. He'd changed a long time ago and she was just now beginning to let herself see the transformation.

The wind blew a gust of cool air from the peaks to the west and north. Elsie felt it lift the hair from her neck. She looked out at the expanse of wildness and wanted to lose herself in it. She turned back and found Corbin watching her. The mountains faded away as she looked at him, and they were teenagers again, the air warm and filled with the smell of the locust trees in bloom along the creek. The beauty of discovering another kindred soul had been intoxicating. She remembered the heady mix of sex, horse shows, and the knowledge she had found her mate. Her trust and assurance in the trajectory of her life had been so steady. And, later, she realized, unfounded.

Magic nudged her hand and she was grounded again in the present. "I would."

Corbin held open the section of fence they had just patched while Elsie led the horses through. On the other side, they mounted and rode through the stretch of tall grass yellowing in the sun. Grasshoppers whirred away from their horses' hooves and disappeared into a thick mat of stems. Away to the left, a lone chipmunk sentinel chirruped a warning of intruders. The horses swished their tails as they climbed out of the grasslands and up toward the heavily forested peaks. Elsie looked over her shoulder and realized they had traveled a great distance from the pastures. Far overhead, a hawk circled, riding the currents of air as they funneled through the mountain pass.

"Do you remember," Corbin said, "that time we drove all night to get to Denver?"

Elsie looked back. Corbin's face was calm but his eyes held the same fire she knew too well. "Yes. We watched the sun come up from the stands outside the stock show."

"Then we went inside and won all our classes and made more money than either of us had ever possessed." His face was that of a boy's again.

Elsie looked away. It was hard to breathe and she felt the bolt of anger in her stomach. That had been one of the happiest days of her life. "I got hurt the very next weekend."

"I know. I thought we had the whole world in our back pocket, Elsie."

The only sounds were the horses' hooves in the tall grass, then the hawk cried out overhead. The small trail forked and instead of going up to the cabin, Elsie urged Magic away into the pine forest. Thimbleberry leaves lined the trail in gold, contrasting with the darker evergreens. She wanted to run and leave Corbin behind. The air was too warm and her head hurt. Her throat tightened and it was hard to swallow. She couldn't have spoken even if she had the words to make Corbin feel how hard the last ten years had been.

"Elsie, can you stop for a minute?"

Still unable to speak, hot tears so close she was afraid to blink, she shook her head and looked straight ahead. The wind combed through her hair, softer now as sunset approached. Magic seemed to sense her anger and pain and was steady under her seat. The trail rose through the pines and the last of the sunlight filtered through, turning the whole world to gold. Finally, Elsie could breathe a little easier. She ran her hand along her leg, thankful that she was able to sit on a horse. She halted Magic and but didn't turn to face Corbin. She felt his leg brush hers as he side-passed his horse up to Magic. He halted as well and Elise looked down at her hands. Their horses stood perfectly still, and their legs brushed through the supple leather of their chaps. Corbin reached across the space separating them and touched her arm so very gently that his fingers felt like bird wings on her bare skin.

"Elsie." His voice was low. The forest around them had fallen silent. No breeze stirred the pine boughs overhead and the woods seemed devoid of animals or birds. The sunlight had turned a rich, saturated gold. Her name hung between them and when she glanced up, quickly, searching his face, she saw so much pain and sorrow.

"I did the most cowardly thing I have ever done, when I left you that morning in the hospital. I'm sorry."

"I know you are." She looked out through the trees. The last of the light made the whole range glow. She felt a little naked without her anger. It was easier, had been easier for a long, long time, thinking that Corbin was a monster. An arrogant and pompous ass was how she had thought of him for a long time. But he had been a boy when he left her. A scared boy. She knew a thing or two about running even though her leg had slowed her down for a while. Now, she felt like she was always running to keep up, or catch up, with her own crazy dreams. Without all the anger, all she had was the truth.

"You hurt me more than I had ever been hurt before." She surprised herself with her own words. She hadn't meant to share so much with him. He grabbed her arm and nearly pulled her off her horse as he held her against his chest. She could hear his muffled sobs as his arms held her so tightly she could barely breathe. When he finally released her, as the horses grew restless beneath them, she knew her own cheeks were wet with tears. His eyes were pure brown and so clear as the tears dampened his long, black lashes.

"Can you trust me again?" he asked.

"I'm trying to figure out how to do that."

"Thank you." He spoke with a depth of heart that made Elsie's chest feel too tight. "I put you in that hospital bed. I was the one who pushed and prodded you into riding that horse."

"I wanted to ride her." Elsie spoke quickly. "I've never blamed you for the accident. It's just the afterward part, when you left.

At that moment, the mustang went stiff between her legs. Elsie looked over at Corbin; his face looked worried as he too felt his horse's fear. He scanned the larger trees higher up the mountain.

"Bear?" she asked.

He shook his head. "I don't know."

Then they saw it at the same time, high in the tree to the west, the sun filtering behind it so that the silhouette was clear: a large mountain lion. It had a fawn, dead and partly eaten and dangling from the tree branches. The horses bolted. Elsie did her best to stay seated, but it took all of her skill to keep herself righted as the terrified Magic raced away from the predator.

"Go to higher ground, Elsie," Corbin shouted.

Elsie and her horse fled up toward the granite rocks and it was not until they were in the open that she was able to look around to see where the lion was. Not following them, she saw that, but where was Corbin?

***

Corbin held his horse back for as long as he could. He could feel all the mustang's muscles coiled beneath him with fear, but he willed the animal to stand its ground. The lion watched from the tree, its tail swishing and eyes catching the light. Thankfully, the large cat did not seem eager to follow them, though Corbin knew to be very, very wary of these magnificent predators. He knew mountain lions were nothing to play with. They were the kind of hunters that tracked and latched onto pray in a stealthy way that made them deadly and hard to predict. He held his horse for one last moment, trying to give Elsie and her mustang time to make it to the granite outcropping.

Finally, he gave his gelding his head. The horse dug his haunches into the soft pine needles and headed for higher ground. The smell of sweating horse mixed with broken pine branches filled Corbin's nose. He bent low in the saddle and steadied the horse as he wove between the trees. The mad rush of adrenaline coursing through his mount's veins made the mustang hard to control. They leaped over a fallen log and as they landed, he felt his gelding lose his footing in the soft pine-needle carpet. The horse faltered, trying to balance his body as one leg caught and the other slid away in the soft earth. Corbin felt a bolt of fear shoot through his stomach; he knew his one-thousand-pound mustang was about to crash to the ground with him upon its back. He tried to push free of the saddle, knowing that he stood a better chance of falling alone than being crushed under his mount's large body. As horse and rider hit the ground, Corbin rolled free, except for his leg. He felt pressure and then a bolt of white pain shot through his leg. He lay still, shocked for a moment as his horse struggled to stand and applied even more pressure to his already trapped leg. Something cold dug into his flesh. He cried out and then forced himself to breathe and stay conscious. The pain was so intense he wanted to vomit. His horse heaved himself up and suddenly Corbin's leg was free. He lay back on the dirt, breathing and trying to focus on the small patch of blue sky overhead. He heard the mustang crashing off into the undergrowth.

He forced himself up onto his elbows. His leg was bleeding and when he carefully pulled his chaps away, he saw blood staining his boot and pant leg. A very old steel fence post was buried in the leaf mold. The tip of the post had impaled his calf. He closed his eyes, thankful that only his leg was injured. Wire twisted around the log he and his horse had jumped. He suspected his horse's leg had caught some of the old barbed wire and that had caused the crashing fall. He inched his body back, using his elbows until he was away from the log and could sit up all the way. He didn't think his leg was broken; after years of training and showing horses he'd had his share of fractures. But he did hurt, bad. He rested on his elbows. Blood seeped from the jagged tear in his flesh.

He heard Elsie's worried call and tried to lie still so that the dizziness would pass and he could answer her. He closed his eyes and concentrated on not blacking out. Once his head had stopped spinning, he yelled as best he could to Elsie. She answered almost immediately.

"Don't ride back. Wait, see if the horses still smell the cat." Even as he shouted out the instructions, he knew she would never listen to him.

A grin spread across his face as he heard the sound of horses in the underbrush. Elsie cantered up and spun Magic in a tight circle. She led Chance by the reins. Her hair swirled loose and long down her back and she wore her tall riding boots and chaps like some sort of western princess. Her face was flushed from the gallop and her eyes were alive with worry. At that moment, he wanted to grab her and kiss her and do even more to her, unfortunately, his leg made it hard to move. She tied off his mustang to her saddle and then her horse to a very solid tree. When she knelt next to him, her hands were trembling and she brushed her fingertips over the tear in his pant leg. He wanted to tell he loved her; he had never stopped loving her. The words wouldn't come as he swirled in and out of dizzy consciousness, and so he closed his lips and let her touch him. Of course, he knew he didn't deserve her care but he would be greedy and take it. He would take all he could and hope she would forgive him along the way. He clenched his jaw as she pulled the torn fabric away from the wound on his leg.

CHAPTER FIFTEEN

"Let me see how bad it is." Elsie worked to gently loosen his boot and then pull it free.

A long, jagged wound ran down the length of Corbin's calf. Elsie took a deep breath and rolled his pant leg up. The flesh was torn and the edges rough, revealing a length of exposed fibula. Her hands trembled as she pulled the fabric away from the seep of dark blood.

"What do you say, Doc?" He was trying to grin. His tone was light even though beads of sweat stood out on his pale forehead, and his eyes were glazed. "You looked a sight galloping down that hill with my horse in tow. I think I should get hurt more often just so you can rescue me."

Elsie tried her best to glare at him. He was attempting to make light of the situation, but right now adrenaline was still coursing through her veins and her pulse was beating so fast in her temples it was hard to focus. At least he was okay. That mattered to her, she realized, very much.

She turned to look at the horses. They both stood calmly. Judging by their relaxed attitudes, it seemed the cat was long gone. Mountain lions were notoriously shy creatures; she imagined it had seen the horses and riders as more of a nuisance than a meal opportunity.

She placed her hands on his leg above the wound. "Does it hurt?"

"Not more than I imagined getting caught on a metal post would hurt," Corbin answered. He was giving her his old cocky grin even though his skin was a shade too light and beads of sweat stood out on his upper lip.

"Okay, sorry. Not the best question," Elsie said. "Do you have any of that whiskey in your saddle bag?"

"No, I forgot to refill after our last camping trip." He was grinning again. Elsie looked down, suddenly wishing that he was not such a man all the time.

She removed the silk wild rag from her neck and tore it into two long strips. Applying even pressure, she bound his leg with economical movements. "Maybe there's something in that cabin back on the ridge? Do you think you can ride?"

"Sure thing," he replied with too much confidence.

It was not a sure thing. Elsie could tell how much it hurt as she helped him first to his feet and then toward his horse. Corbin's face had gone from pale to a weird green under his Lakota summer tan. The back of her throat filled with a bitter taste.

When he grasped a handful of the mustang's mane and was about to swing into the saddle, Elsie urged him to wait. "Gather your strength."

He leaned against the horse for a long moment before looking back at her. He was trying to smile. "Bet you like me better like this, huh?"

"Not particularly." Elsie knew her tone was too sharp but she was nervous and scared. The sun had set and the whole side of the mountain was now in shadow. They had to ride two green mustangs to a hunting shack and she knew Corbin was going to need medical attention soon. She just hoped that they could weather the night and make it to the hospital in the morning.

"You can just leave me here, if you're feeling so put

out." He sounded hurt.

Elsie closed her eyes. Man pride, she thought. Sometimes she forgot that the only person on this earth as stubborn as she was Corbin Darkhorse. "Don't be stupid. Climb up on that semi-broke mustang of yours and let's go spend the night in an abandoned cabin. We can only pray that your leg doesn't get too infected after being sliced open on a fence post, which is probably older than you and I put together."

"Way to cheer me up, babe." He grinned and his face had a touch of color again.

Elsie felt her shoulders relax just a little. "Well, don't faint on me trying to climb on your horse."

"No chance of that. If I pass out, you'd probably leave me for dead."

They were back on familiar ground again.

"Not happening. I need some competition at our mustang championship." Elsie heard his grunt of laughter and so she continued. "I've been waiting for the last two and a half months to see the look on your face when I take home that big check."

"I'm not dead yet, better keep practicing on that half-trained beast of yours."

As the last of the sunlight slipped away, they fell silent. Elsie rode in front and kept looking over her shoulder to make sure he was still sitting his horse. The shadows had lengthened and under the pine trees, night had fully descended. Magic kept his head low and sniffed the ground to find the trail back. Elsie rested her hand on his withers and trusted that he would get them safely out of the woods. Once out of the trees, they rode silently in the moonlight. The high trail was lined with rocks and a few spruces scattered below them. The air was cooler at the higher elevations. Elsie stopped, dismounted, and wrapped her flannel over shirt around Corbin. He tried to argue but she could tell the pain and loss of blood was making him too tired to resist.

At the cabin, she helped him down from his horse and then up the two steps and inside the single-room building. It was pitch-black inside. Elsie hunted for her phone and used the flashlight mode to look around the single room. The floor was relatively clean with only a few dried leaves and pinecone bits scattered across the rough-sawn boards. In the corner, there was a woodstove and plenty of firewood. Next to the east-facing window was a cabinet, and after getting Corbin settled as comfortably as she could on the floor, she rummaged through it. A fully stocked first-aid kit and some cans of soup made her say a fast and silent prayer of thanks to whoever had prepared the cabin. Next to the pile of firewood sat a large canvas sheet and two woven mats. Elsie shook the mats free of dried leaves and then spread them close to the woodstove. She helped Corbin up enough so that he could hobble his way over to them and sit down.

"Are you comfortable enough?" she asked.

"Yes, this is perfect." He nodded at the small cabin.

"Can you hold your phone so that I can use it as a flashlight?"

He took his phone out of his pocket and flipped on the flashlight button. "Too bad we don't have cell service."

She nodded, wishing they could call Bear Dance Ranch or Corbin's mother for help.

"This might burn a little," she said, showing him the bottle of disinfectant and clean gauze.

"Well, I'm sure you'll enjoy it then," Corbin replied.

"Whatever do you mean?" Elsie said. While holding his leg steady, she undid her wild rag from his leg and pulled his boot back off. She worked the torn pant leg up until the long wound was revealed. She poured a liberal amount of antiseptic onto the cotton and then as gently as she could, began to clean around the torn skin.

Corbin was silent and his eyes were closed when she glanced up at his face. His hands were fisted in his lap, the knuckles pale.

"Almost done," she said and retrieved the tube of antibiotic cream.

Once the salve had numbed some of the burn caused by the disinfectant, Corbin winked at her.

"All I meant was," he said, his voice was very low, "I know there have been times when I've made you so mad you have wanted to cut me yourself."

"Yeah, sure. But that's different than enjoying seeing you hurt." Her head was starting to pound. She needed a drink of water and to know everything was going to be okay.

"Well, thanks for taking care of me. And, and I'm sorry about all those other times. I really am," he said.

Elsie looked down at her hands, arranging her face and trying to wipe some of the longing from her eyes. It was better when he acted like a big pain in the behind. When he was nice, she found herself thinking all kinds of crazy things.

"I better get a fire going and the horses watered and settled in for the night," she said in way of answer.

With a fire roaring in the little black stove, the horses tended to for the night, and two cans of some off-brand soup heating, the cabin had taken on a pretty homey feel. Elsie stacked their saddles at the back of the mats and then helped Corbin lean against them. She used the saddle blankets to elevate his injured leg.

A light rain began to fall outside. Elsie checked to make sure the horses were staying dry in the lean-to.

"I'm not sure why I'm worried about them. They are mustangs, after all," she said almost to herself as she closed the door.

"It's your soft heart," Corbin said. "Which I'm very thankful for. I'd have been in a bad way if you had left me out on the trail."

"I couldn't do that," Elsie said.

"I'm sure Eric had a big weekend planned for the two of you. Probably better than this," Corbin said. "You never told me what he did to make you leave so abruptly?"

She took her time answering. "Nothing, really, it was just that I felt like he only liked the idea of me and not who I really am." She hesitated, unsure how much she wanted to reveal to him about her thoughts and desires. She wanted to trust him and feel safe again, and she could remember the way they had been a formidable team together, but that was more than a decade ago and he'd left her when she needed him most.

For a long moment, she imagined what it would have been like to meet Eric's sister and the restaurant where they would have had dinner. She saw the way he would be courteous and careful with her. She could have done it, she could have been the-wife-on-display, but the toll would have been more than that of her accident. She would have been crippling her spirit and selling off her true nature and the essence of who she really was. In the end, all the nice horses, fancy riding clothes, and expensive dinners would never have been enough.

"I wish I could change the past." He looked up at her and his eyes were deep, deep wells of sincerity. "But I can't. I messed up at the worst possible time and now I can understand why Eric would have looked like the safer choice.

"I didn't choose to stay with him." Without thinking, she reached out and touched his shoulder, just wanting to feel his warmth, to feel him. He grabbed her hand, his eyes never leaving her face, and pressed it to his lips.

"I don't want you to compete with Eric." She could hardly swallow; just his lips on her hand sent shivers racing up across her ribs and along her back of her arms.

"Then pick me." He wasn't releasing her hand.

"It's not that easy." She could feel her heart beating with such strength and speed she worried he would feel it through her hand.

"Yes, it is." He lowered his lips again to the hand he held in his own. His eyes were dark and steady as he stared at her.

"No, it's not. I, I really don't know if I can trust you," Elsie said.

He let her hand go and leaned back. "Ahh, there we go," Corbin said. "I deserve that."

"Soup's done." She got up and pulled the heated cans from the top of the stove.

They ate in silence. Somehow, they could go from a raging fire to cold and quiet. The gulf of the past opened and lay between them, dark and sullen on the rough plank floor.

"How bad was it?" Corbin said. "You're so strong now and brave."

Elsie shrugged and took another bite of her soup.

"No, really. Tell me."

She knew he was staring at her, but she didn't want to look up and meet his eyes. "Bad."

A log in the woodstove popped as loudly as a .22 going off.

"I wasn't sure I'd make it out alive. I mean, I wasn't sure I was strong enough, at this one point, to live. I just wanted to give up. Depression does funny things to a person's mind." She wanted to shrug again and change the subject. Drop it. Really, that was what she wanted to do. Just drop the whole stupid business and leave it in the past. That was easier when she wasn't sitting across from the only man she had ever loved. "Everyone kept telling me I should be grateful to be alive. And then, in the next breath, that I'd never ride horses again and I just couldn't wrap my mind around a future without horses." Those had been long, hard days and the nights filled with dreams of wild horses and Corbin and sometimes of the riverbank where they first made love. "I needed you and you left."

There, it was out. The whole truth. She had admitted she needed him. This was different than the blame and anger and the way she had shrugged him off in the past.

"Elsie?"

His voice was soft and so sad. She looked up. He looked young in the light from the candles, a kid again. She wanted to touch his cheek—the way she had when they were teenagers, falling asleep after making love—both had been so amazed at the beautiful thing they had just done, the way they had felt each other's souls while their bodies came together and meshed as one.

"Elsie," he said again. Her name on his lips carried more regret and pain than she had ever heard before. "I'm sorry. Will you let me earn a second chance?"

He stood and limped his way over to where Elsie sat next to the woodstove. He grinned and tried to kneel down, but his leg gave out. Elsie attempted to catch him but he was a tall man and packed with muscle, and so two of them ended up on the floor together. Corbin gasped and beads of sweat again stood out on his forehead. Elsie hurried to stand, but he caught her in his arms and pulled her onto his chest. They lay silent as Corbin's breathing calmed.

"Just lay in my arms," he said. "Don't fight me for once."

Elsie didn't move. Under her hands, she could feel the cords of steel along his abs and her fingers traveled up to feel the sexy groove along his chest. She remembered the night of their impromptu camping trip and the way his skin glistened in the firelight. When she looked up, he was watching her and his eyes were soft and unguarded. Without thinking, she slithered up his chest and rested her elbows beside his face and then bent and kissed him. His arms tightened further around her as he pulled her even closer. His mouth tasted not of the canned stew they had just eaten, but of mint and whiskey and the mountains. She let herself fall into the kiss. His lips were soft and inviting and his tongue toyed with her own so that she felt her whole body melting into his embrace. This was a different

Corbin than she was used to. This man was passionate but not cocky, sexy but not arrogant. Finally, she pulled away, went up for air, and rolled off to lie next to him on the floor. He rolled over to face her, grabbed her hand, and brought it to his lips.

"Will you let me try?" His eyes were still soft. She stared back. "I know you remember how good we were together," he said. "And I don't just mean making love."

Elsie didn't try to deny this. She lay and faced him, letting the pounding of her heart still. Her panties were wet and her whole body wanted nothing more than a night of intense passion with this man. She glanced down and saw his leg had bled through the bandages.

"Oh no, your leg," Elsie said. She sat up and examined the wound.

"Leave it," he said. His voice was low and seductive and his face was a silent plea when she glanced up at him.

"I can't. This is bad," she said.

"I don't care. I just want you, Elsie," he said.

"Corbin, this is serious. I don't have any way to get help, and your leg is really bleeding again," Elsie said.

He rolled to a sitting position and grimaced. Beads of sweat stood out on his forehead again and dark shadows, like reversed hallows, rimmed below his eyes.

"Here, I'll use my belt as a tourniquet," she said.

Elsie went into take-charge-mode. She cleaned the wound as best she could again and put her belt around his thigh to help calm the bleeding, and then she piled wood on the fire and made Corbin a nest from the canvas sheet on which to rest.

He watched her the whole time, his dark eyes slowly growing glazed. She knew the fever was setting in, even if he did not tell her so. Finally, he slipped into a fitful sleep. She sat next to him, touching his damp forehead from time to time with her hand.

CHRISTINA RHOADS

CHAPTER SIXTEEN

As soon as the air outside the cabin was filled with the first trill of morning birdsong and the light had taken on a gray quality, Elsie saddled Magic. She left Corbin asleep on the floor. Below his eyes, large dark shadows made his face look even paler than it should have. Magic was responsive under her seat and legs and left the cabin without even flicking an ear back at the chance. As soon as they both could see well enough to be safe in the predawn gloom, Elsie pushed Magic up into a trot and then canter. Eager to move, he leaped forward. She would have enjoyed the ride, the morning and the connection she had with this previously wild horse so much more if Corbin was not in desperate need of medical attention. If she had known, just a few months ago, that she would be racing toward the rising sun to get help the man who had left her broken in a hospital bed, she would have never believed it. She leaned into Magic's wind-whipped mane and they ran toward civilization and help for Corbin.

She jumped from Magic's back and held his reins in one hand as she banged on Raina's door with her other. The sun had crested the rise to the east and the valley was full of the soft light of morning. Elsie heard noise within the cabin. Raina appeared, her hair disheveled from sleep. "I hoped you two decided to make up and spend a night alone under the stars," she said. "But that's not the case, is it?"

"No," Elsie answered. "He's cut his leg badly and has a fever. He's asleep in the old hunting cabin."

"We'll take the truck." Raina was already turning back into the house, stripping away her night shirt. "There's a road that leads up from the south and we should be able to get most of the way there by vehicle. "Grab my paint mare, with the lightning bolt of white on her hip, and load her up with your mustang. We'll need horses to get him out."

Elsie did as she was told and started the truck once the horses were loaded. Raina motioned Elsie into the passenger seat and then jumped in behind the wheel. "My boys," she said, placing a large medical bag on the seat between them, "seem determined to shorten my life with their antics."

They bounced along a two-track road that Elsie was pretty sure had been designed for horseback riders and not vehicles. They drove until the cabin was nearly in view but a large ridge separated them. Raina stopped the truck. "Horseback from here," she announced.

They saddled the horses, both women efficient and silent as the sun rose fully above the peaks. In another situation, Elsie would have loved the comradery of riding with such a skilled horsewoman. She took a deep breath as she mounted Magic, hoping that Corbin was still sleeping.

***

A pulsing pain pulled Corbin from sleep. He attempted to roll over and was met with a stabbing pain shooting up from his leg. Filtered sunlight came in the tiny window to the east. He took a few deep breaths and then forced himself up onto his elbows. He knew, before he even called her name, that she was gone. It would be fitting, he thought, to wake up to an empty cabin with his leg injured and head pounding. He deserved nothing less. Still, he called out, hoping that perhaps she was just outside with the horses. Silence met his ears. He felt a crooked grin forming on his dry lips. Irony was an understatement. He looked down at his leg. The bandage was darkened with blood, but it did seem to have staunched the flow. He knew he was feverish but he could think, and, he suspected, he could also stand if he tried.

He took his time, easing his weight onto his bum leg. The fire had burned out, but he did see the water canteen sitting next to the firewood. He took the last two swigs and then found his boots. It required more effort than he wished to admit to pull them on. His injured leg no longer wanted to cooperate when he tried to point his toe. He wondered if it was the swelling from infection or perhaps damage to the soft tissue which made it so difficult to move.

The three steps to the cabin door were harder than he had expected. Outside, the light of morning beamed through the pines. His gray whinnied from the pen next to the cabin. "Just you and me, old boy. She left us." He looked off to the south. "Not sure she's coming back either." He rested against the railing, telling himself that he was just assessing the situation, but, truthfully, he was not sure he could saddle his horse and mount on his own. Well, he knew he could if he had to. Men had lived with much worse injuries than his, but it did hurt like hell. Damn, he remembered his saddle was inside, sitting by the woodstove. He pulled himself back into the cabin and hobbled over to retrieve his pile of tack.

Back out in the sunlight, he felt nauseated and lightheaded. Sweat prickled his browline and he knew the fever was heating up again. Chance stood very still as he stumbled into the corral and swung his saddle onto the rails. He had to rest after all that and so he slumped against the gate post. He felt wretched. Not that he needed to feel more remorse for leaving the woman of his dreams injured in the hospital, but still, he knew even with his slight injury how much he would've loved to have her helping him along. Even though he had no right, he remembered the way he had felt that first night away from her. They had been together all summer, traveling around, packing up their horses and gear. Making love in the camper bed with no air conditioning, their bodies slick with sweat. Afterward, they lay together naked, laughing about something, both giddy with pleasure. The sounds of cicadas in the cottonwood trees by the river lulled them to silence. Finally, Elsie moved to rest her head on his chest. He ran his fingers through her hair, untangling the snarls from their romp. A soft rain started to fall. It drummed on the roof of their camper and he pulled her closer to his body. She nestled against him, docile from their lovemaking. He loved these moments when she was calmed from their previous passion and suddenly easy to hold. Not that he wanted a docile woman. Quite to contrary, he loved Elsie's spirit, but when she was soft and gentle, he savored the moments when she let him hold her.

The fever was making the past as real as the present.

He took a deep breath as the mustang nuzzled his arm. That had been a long time ago. Elsie was even stronger now. Last night, for a moment at least, before his leg decided to begin bleeding in earnest, he had thought she would let him make love to her.

The horse nudged his hand. "I bet you'd like a drink of water and some breakfast?" The horse looked at him intently and then perked his ears up and stared to the south. Corbin turned and looked as well. Two riders appeared over the rise. He knew he was not imagining them if the horse saw them too. His eyes didn't want to focus properly but he was pretty sure that one was a black and the other looked a lot like his mother's paint, Moonchild.

"Maybe she hasn't given up on me," he said to the horse. The horse gave him a rather condescending look. The more he worked with these animals the more he was beginning to realize how slow humans really were. "At least we're getting rescued."

The horse whinnied. In an attempt to seem manly, he managed to throw the saddle on his horse. After that effort, he had to lean against the rails again. That was how he was when they rode up. Elsie's hair was loose in the wind and his mother had that look on her face which he had seen too often while growing up.

"Can't you and Clay stay out of trouble?" Raina's face showed displeasure mixed with motherly concern. "I'm getting tired of patching you back together."

"Hi, Mom, it's great to see you as well." He knew he was starting to grin in that silly way, but he had no control. The world was a tiny bit gray at the edges.

Elsie was so beautiful sitting on her horse. He tried to stumble toward the black mustang.

"We better get him on a horse before he passes out," he heard one of the women say. He wasn't sure which one. The world was looking darker and smaller.

CHRISTINA RHOADS

CHAPTER SEVENTEEN

Elsie drove to the hospital, Corbin slumped in the middle between the two women. He was sweating and his skin was pale. He kept his eyes closed and when Elsie touched his arm, he didn't respond.

The nurse on duty greeted Raina by name and immediately put Corbin on a bed with a sheet separating them from the rest of the ER.

"Can you see if my mother is here?" Elsie asked the nurse. "Lina Rosewood?"

"Oh, I think she might be," the nurse replied. "I'll check."

"Your mother works here?" Raina asked.

"She's part of this network and I know she travels to all the hospitals in the region for weekly shortages and training."

"I'd love to meet her." Raina gave Elsie a piercing look. "Especially if this son of mine can convince you to give him a second chance."

Elsie realized her face must have shown her surprise when Raina continued. "Not that he deserves one, a second chance, that is."

The doctor nodded to both women before he

examined Corbin's leg. Corbin was either passed out or asleep, Elsie did not know which.

"He'll live, of course." The doctor winked at Raina.

"I thought as much," Raina replied.

Elsie watched the two banter back and forth like old friends.

"Doctor Fletcher treated both my boys all through childhood," Raina explained.

"Fletcher, this is Elsie Rosewood. She's a mustang trainer and a true force to be reckoned with." Raina smiled with her eyes when she looked at Elsie.

"Oh, yes. I know your mother." The doctor took both of Elsie's hands. "Careful with those wild horses, a dangerous business."

"I know," Elsie said. Her fingers brushed over her thigh of their own accord.

After twelve sutures and a good deal of trimming and debriding, the wound on Corbin's leg looked much better. Raina and Elsie waited outside in the late-morning sunshine.

"I meant what I said inside." Raina spoke slowly, as if choosing her words with great care. "I know Corbin doesn't deserve a second chance with you. I also know he loves you more than he has ever loved anyone, and even more than he loves his own foolish pride. I made mistakes when those boys were young." She paused and looked out at the parking lot and the mountains in the background. "I don't want to make excuses for them, but I do think that if I had done a better job handling the situation with their father that they both would have made fewer mistakes in their love lives."

"They have your last name." Elsie paused. "Don't they?"

"Yes, I did fight for that, at least. Those boys needed a bit of punch to get them started in this world and I thought that would help."

Just then, Lina emerged from the double doors of the

hospital. She silently wrapped her arms around Elsie and pulled her daughter close to her chest.

"I'm fine, Mom." Elsie spoke gently as she unwrapped her mother's arms from around her body. "Corbin has a nasty little gash on his leg, but he's going to be okay."

Raina offered her hand and the two women introduced themselves. Elsie stood by and watched, wondering what her mother was thinking. She knew Lina had not forgiven Corbin for leaving her in the hospital all those years ago. She tried to read her mother's mood as the two older women spoke casually.

Raina broached the awkward subject first. "I know Corbin treated your daughter poorly, very poorly, in the past. But I hope that you might consider giving him another chance, if Elsie decides to try again with that wayward boy of mine."

Lina straightened her back even more and eyed the taller Lakota woman. "Do you know how hard it is to hold your teenage daughter as she cries herself to sleep every night because she has to learn to walk all over again? And the young man, who supposedly loved her, has abandoned her at the first sign of trouble?"

Elsie realized that a great deal of her own fire she came by, quite honestly, came from her mother.

"That sounds heartbreaking." Raina held Lina's gaze and did not look away from the pain and anger so evident on the other woman's eyes.

A warm breeze brought the scent of sap from the copse of red pines next to the parking lot. The three women stood tensed for a couple moments longer, and then Lina relaxed her shoulders and softened her back; it seemed, to Elsie, as if all the pain from the past was slipping from her mother's trim body and away on the soft late-morning wind.

***

Elsie drove the truck and trailer back to Bear Dance Ranch with the mustangs. Raina had suggested she take the horses home and Elsie had willingly left the hospital. She was unsure how to feel about Corbin. So much had changed and shifted over the last few days and she felt as if her whole world had tilted and was unsteady under her feet. The sun was brilliant and as it turned to afternoon. She couldn't remember the sky being so blue. The aspens along the higher ridges were just beginning to turn a brilliant saffron yellow as September crested, and the tamaracks would soon follow. Her whole body eased from its usual tensed stance. She ran her hand absentmindedly down the scar on her leg and it even felt less puckered. The mustang competition was less than a week away and she hoped Corbin would be riding by that time. If he was anything like the young man she had fallen in love with, ten years prior, then he would be grinning and galloping around on his mustang in a few days. She smiled and then realized for the first time in so very long that she was actually thinking about Corbin and feeling an openness of heart. She gripped the steering wheel and guided the truck and horse trailer through the narrow mountain roads toward Bear Dance Ranch.

Clay and Lenora had heard the news about Corbin's accident. Lenora gave Elsie a quick hug. "How was the night?" she asked.

"Long but in some ways just what I needed," Elsie replied.

"He's tough, that little brother of mine." Clay gave Elsie an affectionate squeeze on the upper arm.

"I'm sorry we left you short-handed," Elsie said. "What can I do?"

"Take the guests out riding," Lenora said. "Thanks. Sometimes this all seems so crazy right now." She ran her hand over her stomach. "And the baby isn't even here."

"I'm on it." Elsie fled the ranch house. She needed the fresh air and mountain sunshine to help her think.

***

The next evening, Elsie wiped down the bridles from the guests' horses and pulled fresh saddle blankets out for the morning ride the next day. She was still tired from the previous days' excitement of taking Corbin to the hospital and their long night in the cabin. Thankfully, they gave him some antibiotics and he was already recovering. Raina had sent her a text message that morning saying she would drop her youngest son off at the ranch in the evening. Elsie felt her stomach tighten when she thought about seeing Corbin again. So much had changed for them. Gone was the teenager she had fallen in love with all those years prior, but slowly, she was realizing the man who had taken his place had both depth and courage.

When she turned, Corbin was standing in the doorway. The sun was behind him and she couldn't see his eyes. He moved and took the two strides to reach her. His limp was bad but not stopping him.

"You're back," she said, knowing she was stating the obvious but unable to think as his eyes became clear to her. The expression in them was intense need. She tried to breathe as he reached up and took the last bridle from her hand and hung it on the correct peg, all without taking his eyes from hers. Then he pulled his hat from his head and set it on a saddle behind them. He touched her cheek with the back of his hand, his eyes asking her permission. Then he stepped forward so that she had to look up. Her hips brushed his and his other arm went around her waist, drawing her in so that her hands were pressed against his chest. She took two breaths so shallow they barely counted. He smelled like the forest, like saddle soap. He smelled like honey and wild sage and the mountains. He smelled of home and all the things she loved in this world. Very gently, he ran his thumb along her throat, tipping her chin up. Slowly, he bent his head, his eyes open, watching her. Only at the last second did his eyelids shutter closed.

Elsie felt herself come together as his lips moved against hers, light and so soft. He was not in a hurry, increasing the pressure, encouraging her to open and let him into her soft, wet mouth. Never before had a man kissed her like this, as if he were asking permission to own a part of her. She was scared, delighted, and so turned on.

He pressed the small of her back into him and she could feel his erection through his jeans. Her heart was beating a canter—no, a gallop—of pure, excited need. She wanted this, him. Even if her mind had said no, she would have had to give in to her body's deep, thirsty cry of yes.

He was reading her lips, reading her body. He lifted her up and turned, carrying her to a saddle resting on a stand. He placed her with care upon the oiled leather of the seat. Then he kicked the door closed with the toe of his boot.

With Elsie perched below him on the saddle, he cupped her face with both his hands. He kissed her, deepening until his tongue was stroking hers with the gentle swirls that made her stomach tighten with desire. Then he pulled back, looking into her eyes, and nipped at her lower lip. She moaned, the sound escaping her without permission. A shiver ran up the outsides of her thighs, across her ribs, and settled below the swell of her breasts. He smiled a slow powerful look of ownership and greed and then he grabbed her neck, his fingers loose but firm against her delicate flesh, and kissed her so deeply she could not breathe or think—only feel. When he pulled away, it was to struggle out of his shirt and then he was back for more, wringing his hands around her neck, stroking down her shoulders, and kissing her ever deeper. His fingers struggled with the buttons on her shirt. He nipped her lip again when she tried to help, and he placed her hands around his neck. But she wandered. His shoulders were broad, muscled, and she wanted more. She stroked down his back, along his stomach, and let her hands fall to rest on his belt buckle.

"What do you want? Elsie, tell me what you want from me." He spoke slowly, his voice barely more than a hungry whisper against her neck.

"I want," Elsie said. She could barely breathe; his lips sent rings of sensation vibrating out through her body as he kissed her exposed skin.

"Yes?" he said. His voice was no more than a whisper, moving the hair off her neck.

"I want you to make love to me," she said. "Like before."

He pulled back, holding her chin with his thumb and cupping her cheek in his roughened palm. His eyes were dark but open. He was asking her questions, seeing her. She felt his attention and patience and under it all, his hungry lust.

"Corbin, I want you to make love to me like before. The way you did when we were too young to know better. The way you did before you left." There, the truth was out. There was no going back now, no hiding behind her old anger, frustration, and hurt anymore.

CHAPTER EIGHTEEN

"My love," Corbin whispered into her hair as he held her head against his chest. "I will."

How long had he wished and wanted for this time to come and for her to give him another chance. He was slow as he bent his head and nuzzled her lips with his own. When he pressed her gently, she opened her mouth and he took his time, letting his tongue wander over hers, stroke and tease until she was soft and pliable in his hands. He pulled her shirt over her head, only lifting his lips from hers for the briefest moment as her top slid off. Then he slipped her bra off and sighed as he cupped her small, shapely breasts in his hands. He dropped to his knees, looking up at her and running his hands over her beautiful body. He carefully took one nipple in his mouth and ran his tongue over it in slow, meandering circles. Her head fell back and she arched beautifully, still perching on the saddle. He looked up and ran his hands over her gorgeous sides. He hardened further as he realized he could give this wild woman some pleasure.

He stood, needing her to be closer, and kissed her mouth. Biting her lower lip so hard he tasted blood, he fisted his hands in her wild mane and pulled her head back and looked into her eyes. Never had he dreamed that he would be given the opportunity to once again pleasure this willful and headstrong woman. He struggled with the buckle on his pants, worried she might change her mind, like she had that night as they camped. Somehow, he had to show her that he was worth a second chance—he planned to use his whole body to convince her.

Her hands wandered up his neck and she smiled and touched his cheek. His heart beat unsteadily in his chest. She was soft and glowing in the last of the golden light from the sunset. He stopped with his pants and cupped her face in his hands, kissing along her lips with delicate tiny kisses before taking her lower lip in his teeth and then sucking, eliciting a moan from her throat that sent a shiver down his spine. He pulled her to her feet and undid the button on her jeans and stripped her down, revealing her long, lean thighs. He couldn't help it and fell to his knees in front of her. The scar on her leg was darkened and raised and ran nearly the whole length of her thigh. Higher above her femur scar, several whiter incision sites dotted her hip in uneven rings. His breath was unsteady as he slipped her underwear down and ran his thumb over her skin. He kissed along the raised scar and then carefully gave each smaller mark his full attention. Silently, he spoke words of thanks that he could touch her now, years later. Somehow, he would heal the past with his tongue, his lips, his whole being. Her body melted under his mouth and he felt her skin grow warm and moist. He should have done this years ago, when all the marks were so fresh. He knew that he would live with that regret forever, yet, forward was his only chance at salvation and forgiveness.

Her hands running through his hair, fingers restless and filled with need, focused him back on the task of seduction. She was bare under his hands and mouth, and needy. She rocked against him, her hips brushing his arms and sending shivers through his whole body. He bent his head and touched his hot and hungry mouth to her exposed labia. She moaned and grabbed his head even harder, grasping fistfuls of his hair and drawing him closer to her. He took this as a sign she enjoyed his tongue and so he suckled on her exposed clit and brushed his fingers over her, drawing the folds of her labia back so that his tongue could circle over her. She moaned and gasped and he felt a jolt of pure, male pride to hear the woman he desired so strongly enjoying his attention. He was having trouble thinking. When he stood, the room had disappeared around them. He let his hands grasp her buttocks and he lifted her off the saddle just enough to position her hips. She undid his belt buckle and he felt the backs of her hands brush the skin of his stomach. His whole body felt as if it were quivering with need and he had to grit his teeth when she freed him from his jeans.

"Darling, I have a condom somewhere. Maybe my pocket?" He knew his voice was raspy, heavy with lust.

She kissed his neck and then produced a foil packet and slid the prophylactic over his damp and erect head. The touch of her fingers along the length of him made him moan and close his eyes. With all necessary precautions taken care of, he let himself go and rocked and lifted her back in the saddle until he could rest the head of his penis against her wetness. He kissed her, stroking his tongue over hers, and then pulled away, wanting to see the look in her eyes as he entered her. Gently, he pushed into her folds and felt her body welcome him even as she gasped. He held her gaze, watching her eyes as they widened.

"Elsie." He just needed to say her name aloud.

She grasped the back of his neck, pulled his face toward hers and kissed him with such desperate need he could no longer hold back. He rocked against her hips, used all the skills he had learned in the saddle to try to pleasure this woman he so desired. Her growl in his ear made his stomach tense and he thrust into her again and again. She ran her nails down his back and he tried to tell her how much he loved her, tried to show her with all his man*ness* how much she meant to him, how much he needed her. He was glad he could finally show her. She held all the power over him, always had. He was a fool to think he could live without her.

"Elsie, you beautiful, sexy woman," he whispered into her ear as he pulled her even closer. When he pulled away from her kisses, he could see the glaze of desire in her eyes. His heart was pounding; she wanted him as much as he wanted her. How had he been so lucky to meet and tame this wild creature? He kissed along her throat and felt her body open even further to him, so he buried the head of his cock as deep into her softness as he could and then ran his fingers over her aroused clit. She gasped and tilted her pelvis into his hands, and so he pinned her against the saddle with his manhood and pleasured her with his fingers. He couldn't think of any place he would rather be than with this goddess with her wild hair. He thrust gently, knowing he was so deep inside her, and was rewarded by her cries of pleasure coming faster and closer together. Then he felt her tighten her deep, deep muscles around his cock, and her head rolled back as the orgasm rocked through her body. He kissed her, wanting to absorb some of her pleasure even as he finally let the steely grip he held on his own desire loosen enough so that he thrust into her and found his own hot and fast relief. He kissed her and rocked against her long after they had both been sated, before sliding to the ground to carefully cradle her naked body against his. He wanted nothing but to hold her and prolong the beauty of their two joined bodies. The world could wait, the world be damned. He had finally made love to his lady and he wanted nothing but to hold her and breathe in her scent and taste the salt on her lips.

She lifted her tousled head from his chest.

"Wow," he whispered.

A smile danced across her lips and her cheeks turned pink.

He felt his own face smiling, no, grinning, back at her.

She was beautiful and sexy with her dark eyes sated and her hair a mess. He was afraid to move too quickly and scare her off, or anger her. He ran his thumb across her lips. They looked red and like they had been kissed too much. He felt warmth low down in his stomach, realizing he'd made them look that way.

"I wanted to do this in the cabin two nights ago," he said. His voice sounded hoarse even to his own ears.

"I know you did. But you were quite literally bleeding out on the floor." She raised her head and rested her chin on her hand so that she was eye level with him. "How's the leg, by the way? Did you open up the sutures?"

He wanted to squeeze her and tuck her head into his chest, but he knew she needed her space and so settled for running his hands across her bare back.

"Thanks for saving me." He tried to wink. "And the leg is fine, still attached and everything."

She grinned, showing off her dimple and he just stared, still amazed she was in his arms.

"I had to keep you alive," she replied. "I need some competition."

He could not resist any longer, he pulled her against his chest and held her as if she were one of the wild horses and might run off. He knew deep down that he would have to give her space, not pressure her too much. She was the kind of woman who needed to be wanted, loved, but not held too tightly. He knew this about her. Now that he had her back, he would do anything to keep her, anything. He kissed her forehead, and her skin smelled of sunshine and wind and the sweetness of her sweat.

"Elsie," he said her name and she looked up at him. Her eyes were dark brown and soft like he hadn't seen them in years. "I love you more than anything on this earth." He paused, watching her eyes widen further. He half expected her to look down and away and close off from him again. He would have deserved that; he knew this and was ready. Instead, she brushed her hand across his cheek. "I know you do." She ran the tip of her tongue across her lips. "I'm learning how to forgive you. If I hadn't loved you so much back then, it wouldn't have hurt so bad when you left." She shifted onto her elbows so that she was above him. He ran his hand through her hair, pulling it away from her face. "I'm scared to give you that kind of power over me again."

His throat closed and he pulled her back down against his chest and kissed the top of her head, burying his face in her tangled hair. "I'm sorry. I won't ever leave again. I promise." He hoped she felt the weight of truth in his words. "I would die before ever leaving you again. If you can forgive me, just a little, I'll prove my trustworthiness to you every day."

"Okay," she breathed against his chest. "I'll try."

He placed a thumb under her chin and tilted her head up so that he could kiss her lips again.

They lay still in each other's arms, the outside world still distant. The horse blanket was scratchy but he did not want to relinquish her.

From his chest, she spoke, her breath warm. "We should get dressed. I hardly want to be found naked in the tack room."

"Yes." He didn't want to agree.

Letting her go, leaving this moment behind, wasn't what he wanted. He also could picture Clay walking in on them and then giving him a long lecture on how to treat a lady. Clay didn't understand that Elsie had not given him much room for planning. He was trying to keep up with her, and when she let him touch her, he was not about to say no and foolishly recommend a bed.

He willed his finger to open and her soft skin slipped away from his.

***

Later, at the dinner table, Elsie looked up and found

Corbin's gaze on her. She felt warmth flood her cheeks as she pictured his bare chest under her hands and then she blushed even more as she remembered the way she had dug her fingernails into his firm behind.

"You two are awfully quiet tonight," Clay said between mouthfuls.

Lenora looked up and smiled. "And Elsie is blushing," she observed.

Corbin began to grin.

"Did you work everything out?" Lenora asked. "Did a night in the wilds with an injured leg give the two of you enough time to make up?"

"Yes," Elsie said. "Sorry about before. We just needed to really understand each other."

Clay began to laugh. "You're something else, Elsie," he said. "Corbin, you better be careful. The last girl I met with that much heart I had to marry."

Corbin looked directly at Elsie and smiled very slowly. She felt herself blushing and stuck her tongue out at him. He winked and a shiver ran up her ribs and made her heart beat a little faster.

"Are the two of you ready for the Championship this weekend?" Byron cut through the dinner-table flirting.

"Yes, Sir." Elsie set her fork down and smiled. "Magic handled our mountain adventure like a pro."

"If this leg of mine cooperates, Chance and I should be ready to give Miss Rosewood a run for her money." Corbin grinned even wider as he watched Elsie's face.

"Don't use that leg as an excuse, Corbin." She knew he was baiting her, but she couldn't help herself.

"We can't wait to see both of you," Lenora said. She pattered her round stomach. "I think the baby will like her first mustang training competition."

"Three more weeks and we get to meet her." Clay took his wife's hand and gently kissed each knuckle. Elsie looked down as Lenora brushed her hand over Clay's cheek. When she looked back up, Corbin was watching her and his eyes were so soft that her breath caught in her throat.

CHAPTER NINETEEN

The day of the Mustang Challenge dawned clear and cool. Elsie drove the ranch truck with Lenora, Annie, and Byron, while Clay and Corbin drove the horse trailer in front. There was little traffic on the roads as the sun began to rise to the east. Lenora had been feeling a little tired and nauseous since Elsie had returned from her mountain misadventure with Corbin and so every waking second Elsie had been helping out with the guests, cooking, and preparing the ranch for their leave. There had not been a free minute for her and Corbin and a sort of shyness had developed between them. Elsie caught him smiling at her but with all of their old angry banter no longer needed, they were tongue-tied around each other.

She took a deep breath and steadied her hands on the steering wheel. Last night, she had barely slept. When she finally drifted into a fitful sleep, she had been plunged into a dream in which she was standing in the clay arena in Denver. The wild filly shivered and shied away from her hand as she reached out to touch the horse's damp shoulder. The dream shifted and changed shape and then she was riding Magic up the side of a steep shale slope. The loose scree kept falling from under his hooves and he struggled to stay upright beneath her. She had woken abruptly and got out of bed. Hurriedly, she opened the door on her small trailer to peer into the darkness. She'd needed to assure herself that her black horse was indeed peacefully eating hay in the predawn light.

Clay and Corbin pulled the horse trailer into the large parking lot next to the barns and arena, and Elsie followed them. Her stomach clenched so tightly around the small breakfast, which she had struggled to choke down before leaving the ranch, that she worried she might be sick in the gravel lot. She took a couple deep breaths and reminded herself she had been preparing for this day for the past ten years.

Lenora squeezed her arm but didn't speak. Elsie tried to give the other woman a reassuring smile but her lips felt too stiff to move.

Outside the vehicle, the cool air of the morning made it easier to breathe. She opened the trailer door while Corbin and Clay unloaded the hay and water buckets for the horses.

Corbin touched her shoulder. "Are you okay?" He spoke close to her ear so no one else could overhear them.

"Yes." She made her voice sound firmer than she felt on the inside.

"We don't have to do this."

She glanced at him and realized that his face also looked pinched and his eyes worried. Part of her wanted to wrap her arms around him and feel his reassuring strength, the other part wanted to say something rude, start an argument and then use it as a distraction. She decided that was the old her.

"Corbin, I'll be fine." She moved into the horse trailer to unload the mustangs. "This isn't like last time." She spoke to as much to reassure herself as Corbin. "I'm prepared, the horse is prepared. This is all new." Hopefully, her words were true.

"I know…" He stood silhouetted in the horse trailer

door. "You, Elsie, are going to shine today."

***

Corbin commanded his heart to slow down; as he gave her a leg up, his hands were shaking. Elise looked down at him for a brief moment. Her face was pale and he could see the fear of failure in her eyes. "You got this." He spoke quietly so that only she could hear. "You've waited a long time for this day. Go out there and ride your wild horse. Show the world how amazing you are, Elsie Rosewood. Show them your wild heart."

She smiled and ran her fingers through her horse's mane. The music started and Corbin stepped away. This was so different, he reminded himself, from the terrible clay rodeo area in Denver. He could still smell the sweating horses, their fear evident, and hear that raucous music. This was all new. He could smell the tamaracks lining the creek just south of the big arena and the wind brought the clean air of the mountains down. He rubbed his damp palms along his jeans. His ride would be a little after hers, but he knew she would win with the high score. He could feel it in the air. She and that black mustang were bonded in such a unique and beautiful way.

No matter how much he would've liked to keep Elsie safe, she wanted this, she wanted it with all her heart. He had to let her have her way. He just hoped there would be enough of her heart left for him to have a piece to call his own. But for now, he would cheer her on, worry less about her safety, and instead appreciate the talented horsewoman she truly was. He knew she was better with the animals than he. Maybe, together, they could become a team: he would entertain the people, make jokes, recite poetry, and Elsie could show the people the magic of connection. He almost laughed out loud. *The Magic of Connection* was exactly what they would call their clinics. After all, he reasoned, they had learned to connect with each other even though the past was against them.

The music, the black horse, and Elsie's concentrating face had the whole crowd mesmerized. Corbin looked around to see the expression of wonder on peoples' faces. She and Magic where something to see: no leather, steel, or rope separated the two from each other. Without a saddle or bridle, Elsie rode her formerly wild horse into the arena and captured the attention of every person in the stands. The music paused and the mustang gathered his haunches to begin his first spin.

When Elsie glanced up from her horse, their eyes locked and Corbin felt a smile of pure admiration and pride pull his lips up. He nodded to her and she flashed him a quick smile of her own. He saw that she was beginning to relax and enjoy the moment. Magic looked perfectly calm and at ease with the whole performance. On horseback, she was a princess, a warrior. She was riding into battle or into the future. He couldn't tell which, but he was just as spellbound as everyone else. Slowly, she moved the horse into a canter; she kept her hands steady on his neck as she asked for him to change leads again and again. She directed her horse toward the obstacle in the middle of the arena and the pair easily sailed over it. The crowd exploded. But Elsie and Magic were not done. The music slowed and they stopped in the middle until a crescendo built and built and the black horse reared high in the air. He balanced on his haunches, his powerful hindquarters carrying all of his weight and that of his rider as well, then, slowly; he pawed the air and settled back down on all four feet. Elsie cued him into a bow and he lowered his head down to the arena footing, his left front leg bent underneath him.

Corbin clapped along with everyone else. Elsie was smiling as she looked up and searched for Corbin in the crowd. He raised his hand and blew her a kiss and she smiled before turning and galloping out of the arena.

Outside, a soft rain was falling and she slipped off of

Magic. Corbin caught her in his arms. He wanted to tell her how proud he was that she had trained this wild horse, but instead, all he could do was silently hold her and breathe in her scent. A reporter was behind them, and he could hear the man clearing his throat. All he wanted to do was whisk her away, keep this woman all to himself. Instead, he let her go, let his arms slip from around her.

He turned to the reporter. "Elsie's technique is called *The Magic of Connection* and it's a way for humans and horses to work together. And it's all about mutual respect and understanding. In fact, it's the best way for people to understand their horses, and maybe a little about themselves along the way."

"Wow, big endorsement coming from Corbin Darkhorse," the reporter said as he quickly jotted down the statement.

Katie from *Western Horsemen* approached as well. "Great ride, Elsie. Truly inspirational. Can we talk about doing a feature shoot with you next week?"

A group of young girls gathered around the horse and rider. "Can you teach us how to ride like that?" one asked.

Elsie smiled a quick thanks to Corbin and then turned to the reporters and young girls. She was calm and steady and kept her smile on. Corbin walked away, leaving her to the adoring fans that had begun to throng around the mustang and horsewoman.

"Mustangs are amazing animals," he heard her say. "They are part of our heritage and their way of life is at risk. They, just like us humans, need a little freedom in order to truly thrive."

CHAPTER TWENTY

She heard him at the door before he even knocked. Lying still in bed, she could almost feel him standing in the dark just outside her door. His knuckles were hesitant, dragging for an inch or two after they rapped. She waited; her breath catching in her throat and heart galloping a fast beat in her chest. Her feet felt numb as she climbed down from the bed. Her hands fumbled with the catch on the door and then silver light from the stars spilled into the darkness of her trailer. He was a darker silhouette against the stars and sky, and she touched his shoulder and then face. He stood still while her hand moved across his cheek, then he pulled her against him. The grass was dewy on her bare feet and she gasped as he lifted her up. His jeans were rough on the insides of her thighs as she wrapped her legs around him. Under her nightshirt, she was bare and she heard his indrawn breath as his hands moved from her hips to her bare buttocks and then to caress down to the place where leg and body joined.

He carried her to the corral gate and perched her gently on the wood. Then his hands cupped her face and he kissed her so deeply she had to cling to him or lose her balance and fall from her high seat. He unbuttoned his belt with one hand and caressed the length of her thigh with his other hand, all the while kissing her until he knew she was completely his and his alone.

"Elsie," he whispered, pulling back. "I came to talk to you."

"Can it wait?" She spoke between the small nips she gave his neck.

"Yes," he growled.

He pulled her down just a little until she could feel the press of his erection still cased in his jeans. Sweat prickled along her hairline and she felt goosebumps tighten the skin across her ribs and make her nipples harden. He kissed her deeper, his tongue needy and hot in her mouth. He shifted between her legs and she felt his pants slip down further. She pushed against him, wanting to feel his man*ness*. He rewarded her by freeing himself fully from his clothes. He tipped her back just a little and then rested the tip of his erection against her wetness. He kissed her mouth and then pulled back.

"I love you." His voice was low.

A soft breeze brought the scent of honeysuckle. Elsie shivered against Corbin, something shifting deep inside her heart. "I love you too," she whispered back.

He bent and kissed her again as he pushed into her. Her whole body tingled with his penetration. All of her senses came alive as she ran her hands over his back and tasted the mint on his breath. Her own breathing sounded ragged to her ears and she arched her back to meet his thrusts.

"You feel amazing," he choked. "Can we go to your bed?"

Without waiting for her answer, he pulled her from the rail and carried her into her horse trailer.

The room was in shadow and he didn't bother to close the door. She kissed him hungrily, missing the fullness of him inside her. He tossed her onto the rumpled bed she had left not long before. He pulled off his pants and tore the shirt from his body. She caught flashes of his naked skin, scored by moonlight and illuminated in snatches. Naked, stripped down, and so very hard, he stood before her. She began to slip her night shirt over her head but he stopped her, catching her arms above her head and pulling the garment off. He ran his hands down her sides. Taking his time, letting his thumbs follow the curves of her breasts and then brush across her sensitive nipples. He followed her body down. With deliberate slowness, he moved across her hips and then thighs before dipping down to the place between them. He didn't touch her clit immediately; instead, he bent his head and ran his tongue over her exposed labia. She choked, the jolt of pleasure sending her nerve endings rattling and jumping.

"Do you like this?" He spoke against her flesh, barely breathing the words. His lips felt damp and hot and so very close to her very intimateness.

"Yes." Her whole body was humming with his touch.

"Good." That was the last he spoke.

She clutched the bedsheets. Her body had gone soft as his tongue stroked up, teasing her. It felt as if she were riding on a knife edge of pleasure so long and deep, she feared the fall on either side. With her left hand, she released the sheet and grabbed a fistful of his black hair. He alternated between circling around her clit in broad tongue-sweeps and suckling her in such a way that her calves trembled. Slowly, he increased the speed and depth. When she thought she could not take any more, he slid his tongue over her quickly and she felt a surge of pleasure so intense she knew she could never recover. Lost, completely out of control, she let her body rush toward the salvation he held. She thought for a brief moment, before she came, that she might lose herself irrevocably in this man, and yet, she knew her choice had been made years ago, and so she let go and fell toward all he offered.

They lay in her bed. He held her as she trembled, her

head resting on his chest and body, spent from the shock of pleasure that had just coursed through it. He ran his hands over her back, stroking her skin to gently bring her back to this world. She could hear the wind whining around the eaves of the trailer. The soft spatter of first raindrops brought the smell of dust turning back to rich earth. Corbin started to get up to close the open door.

"Leave it," she whispered.

He settled back into her bed and drew her close, kissing the top of her head. They lay in silence and listened to the rain go from a patter to a downpour. The world seemed to be wrapping them in the softest of watery veils. Slowly, with the passage of time and the easing of her body, she felt Corbin drawing near to her in a way she had not felt since they were young and completely naïve to the path ahead.

The rain steadied and then ushered them both into sleep.

***

Elsie woke with the light to find herself naked in her bed. Corbin lay next to her. She thought back on the previous night. Her face heated when she remembered his mouth upon her damp body. She ran her fingers over his chest. He had pleasured her and then held her until she slept and never once tried to initiate more. Slowly, he opened his eyes. The smile that spread across his face and filled his sleepy eyes with joy made her heart surge with happiness. He pulled her against him once more, kissing her head and touching her face with his fingertips.

"Good morning, my love." His words felt like coming home.

"Let's do this every morning for the next fifty years." She spoke without thinking, for once her heart and mouth linked perfectly.

"Really?" Corbin pulled her toward him so that she was

216

nestled under his chin. "You're giving me a second chance?"

"I'm giving *us* a second chance."

"Good." He spoke against her neck as he pulled her astride him. Her hair was wild and loose. He knotted his hands in it and pulled her down so that he could kiss her swollen lips.

CHRISTINA RHOADS

EPILOGUE

The sun had not yet risen and a chill predawn gray held the world in suspended rest for a little longer. Corbin watched the way she sat on her mustang, back straight and shoulders pulled back. She was perhaps more Joan of Arc than cowgirl, and he could all too easily imagine her leading a legion of troops into battle. He felt his throat tighten with joy and love and deep respect. This was her idea, of course, but he had gladly driven the eight hours in the dark to make it happen. Chance was eager under his seat, the horse's gray ears pointed forward and large nostrils took in the scent of crushed sage, sand dust, and pungent juniper. As they crested the rocky rise, the sun began to send out tendrils of light and suddenly the horizon was lightened to a blue as soft and delicate as a songbird's egg. She looked back at him and then waited, and together they watched the sun lighten the sky to gold and then orange before the blue of the morning made the whole world come alive. Down below and off to the east was one of the only springs in the whole stretch of arid land. A herd of ten or twelve mustangs grouped around the tiny oasis. Magic's ears were locked on the small moving band of horses and Chance tracked them as well.

Carefully, Elsie slid from her horse's back and Corbin followed suit. They pulled the halters from their horses and then stood in silence, the mustangs free and yet still sharing space with the humans. He saw Elsie rest her hand on Magic's shoulder. He knew that she wanted nothing more than to take her wild horse back home and yet she also wanted him to choose her.

When a horse below them lifted its head and whinnied, it was as if a spell had been lifted and their two mustangs shot down the steep slope, tails flying out behind them and catching the morning light. Elsie stepped into his side and he put his arm around her, drawing her against him. He could feel that she was breathing quickly and her shoulders felt tight and high as they poked into his ribs. He kissed the top of her head, thankful that she wanted to be near him.

A tall roan with flaxen mane and tail charged at the two newcomers but then eased back as a lean gray mare stepped forward. Both Chance and Magic sniffed noses with the gray horse; she had a leggy yearling at her side.

"Could that be their mother?" Elsie's voice was little more than a whisper.

"Maybe."

They watched as the two newcomers shifted in next to the gray mare and all the horses headed toward the springs. He could feel that Elsie wanted to both leave and stay, and so he undid his backpack and pulled out a thermos of coffee and sack full of trail mix. They sat on the rock huddled together and silent, watching the horses drink and eat the tall grass next to the spring, then the large roan pushed them away and Corbin saw a dark shadow hiding next to a large outcropping of rock.

"There's the mountain lion."

The herd spooked and fled into the rocks and sage. The sun rose higher. Corbin set up a sunshade using a piece of canvas as the frost of the morning burned off and the rocks began to heat. They waited, talking of the future and planning a series of clinics. The winter would be busy but they would return to Bear Dance Ranch in the spring to help with the influx of guests. Slowly, the sun inched across the sky and there was no sign of the herd of horses. Another smaller band came down to drink after midday, but they did not linger either. The mountain lion was nowhere to be seen but Corbin imagined that it must be close.

"He keeps the mustang numbers in check," Elsie said as if reading his mind. The BLM doesn't plan to do a round-up here next year."

"I know it might seem callous to say, but I'd rather that the horses have a natural predator than be rounded up and shipped off."

"Me too. The first time I saw Magic in the pen at the holding facility, I was shocked by how terrified and angry he was. The whole experience of being separated from their family and shipped away is very hard on the horses."

Corbin smiled and grabbed her hand. "I'll never forget how my heart started beating when I realized the gorgeous cowgirl in front of me was you."

Elsie looked down, blushing suddenly. He cupped her chin in his palm and lifted her face until he could see her eyes. They were clear and a little bright with unshed tears.

"You wanted to kill me." He spoke slowly, watching her face and luxuriating in the feel of her skin under his fingers.

"I did." She smiled and her eyes flashed with such fierce independence that his breath caught in his throat.

Later, she was quiet as they watched a hawk circle high in the sky. He could tell she had given up hope. "Let's wait a little longer." He kept his tone light and she nodded. They napped in the warmth of the sun, both exhausted from their all-night drive to reach the birthplace of their mustangs.

But when the sun was setting, they had to make their

way back to the truck and horse trailer. It was only a couple of miles, but at night, it would hardly be ideal terrain with the rocks and drop-offs.

They walked slowly, in silence. Corbin prayed; in his head. He tried to picture the horses turning, lifting their heads, and then returning, looking for the humans who had become trusted partners in life. With his whole being, he wanted Magic to come back to the woman he loved, they both loved. He knew the mustang loved her; that had been evident in the way he trusted and responded to her every direction.

Much later, the truck in sight, he stopped Elsie and pulled her against his chest. He knew she was silently crying.

"I'm sorry," he whispered.

"Thank you." She spoke carefully.

He looked up at the setting sun off to the west. The whole valley was consumed by a purple shadow. On the ridge above them, he thought he saw movement. When he looked again, purple silhouettes stood out, following the trail on which they had just walked.

"Elsie, look." He turned her in his arms so that she too could see the dark outlines.

"It can't be them." Her voice was too high and she leaned away from him.

The silhouettes dropped down from the high ridge and then were lost completely in shadow. It was not until they were very close that Corbin could tell they were, in fact, horses.

"Corbin," she breathed out his name. "It is them."

The hairs on the back of his neck stood up. The two mustangs trotted toward them, ears pricked forward. Elsie began to laugh and then cry as he hugged her, his own face tracked with tears. The two horses stopped in front of them, licking and breathing hard from their journey. Their eyes were bright and they leaned forward to nuzzle at Elsie and then him. Corbin stared in amazement as Magic licked

Elsie's face. She began to laugh in earnest, closing her eyes, and Corbin watched her and felt his own laughter bubbling up from deep in his soul. It was as if the last ten years of guilt and mistakes were forgiven wholly. When she opened her eyes, she smiled at him and she was soft and warm and once again the guileless young woman poised to take on the world.

"Will you marry me, Elsie?" He spoke slowly, trusting that she would not close off from him again.

Her eyes grew very large and he saw her mouth move and then her brows draw together, but she did not speak. He smiled, proud that he could still render her speechless. He took full advantage of the moment and sank down to one knee. With both of his hands, he grasped her fingers and looked up at her. She was biting her bottom lip and looked like she was about to cry again and so he spoke hurriedly.

"Elsie, I love you and I have from the very first moment I saw you sitting on your pretty gelding. I want to marry you, if you'll have me. I promise I'll never leave you again and that I'll drive you crazy, make love to you like you're the only woman in the world, and ride all the wild horses right beside you."

She was silent and tears filled her eyes, but she didn't look away from his face. He could tell she was searching his soul, trying to discern whether or not she should trust him with the rest of her life. "I know I'm asking for a lot. I know that I'm asking for everything. But, Elsie, I love you and we belong together. We are perfect together, and so, will you please marry me?"

"Yes. Yes, Corbin, I will." She was crying and he wanted to hug her to him but he had to fish the chain from around his neck and the tiny silver ring with the chunk of turquoise.

"I can get you a real diamond," he said, holding it out and then slipping it on her finger. "If you like? It's old and from my mother's family and I know it might not mean a lot to you..." He knew he was babbling now and thankfully she pulled him back up to his feet and kissed him.

"I love it," she whispered.

With Elsie's arms around his neck and two mustangs suddenly curious about their humans' embrace, Corbin was surrounded by those he loved.

Her lips were hot and wet and tasted of salty tears and the promise of a whole lifetime with the most stubborn and wild-hearted woman he had ever met.

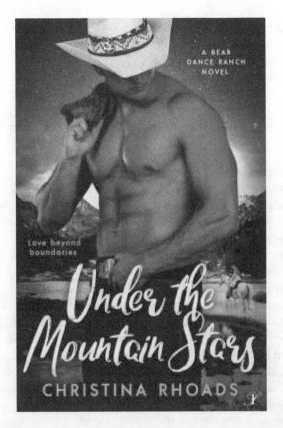

After the death of her mother and end to her troubled marriage, Lenora Ranvier is feeling more alone than ever before. She takes her aunt and uncle up on their offer to come and live on their failing cattle ranch in the Montana Mountains.

Lenora hopes to grieve and start over but has no plans to fall in love again. All that changes the moment she meets Clay Darkhorse, Lakota cowboy and foreman of Bear Dance Ranch.

Clay knows Lenora is the woman for him as soon as he sees her climb out of her pickup truck, exhausted and beautiful. He slowly wins over Lenora by taking her on long night horseback rides into the starry mountains but both Lenora and Clay have past traumas to heal before they can freely love again.

Joining forces they convert the ranch from a struggling cattle operation into a swanky guest resort. But Lenora and Clay must learn to trust each other if they are to share a love as true and strong as the mountains in which they live.

Excerpt:

Despite the slow pulse of a headache, Lenora did not want to leave Clay. What she really wanted was to sit with him quietly, to show him she loved him more than she feared a broken heart. She needed a quiet night to say those words to him; a night to ride in the mountains, to feel the brush of stars and the smell of pine sap on the breeze. Instead, she went to his bedside, and with the nurse, his mother, her aunt, uncle and his brother all watching she bent and kissed his pale lips. When she pulled back his eyes were open, and that half smile she so loved slowly appeared on his face.

"Maybe I should tell those young colts to try and kill me more often." Clay said. "Seems you like me better hobbled and in bed."

Was it her imagination, she wondered, or was he flirting with her in front of his mother. Her face was hot, and she could not look up from the bedsheet.

"Please, don't ever let it happen again," Lenora said..

Available at all major retailers.

ABOUT THE AUTHOR

Christina Rhoads resides on an Arabian horse farm where she divides her time (when she isn't fixing fence or stacking hay) between writing novels, painting and training equines. While studying creative writing as she earned a BA in English from Indiana University, she fell madly in love with the act of creating characters and then sharing them with the world.

She often describes her ideal afternoon as one spent riding her horse, Major Temptation, and then curling up with a good book and cup of peppermint tea.

For more on Christina's books check out her website or connect with her on social media.

www.christinarhoads.com

https://www.facebook.com/Christina-Rhoads-212417315991236/

https://www.instagram.com/christina.rhoads.author/?hl=en